**PURE
SLUSH
BOOKS**

SLOTH

7 Deadly Sins Vol. 4

First published as a collection November 2018

Pure Slush Books
32 Meredith Street
Sefton Park SA 5083
Australia

Email: edpureslush@live.com.au
Website: https://pureslush.com/
Store: https://pureslush.com/store/

Original coffee stain image copyright © magicmarie
Cover design copyright © Matt Potter

ISBN: 978-1-925536-66-9

Also available as an eBook
ISBN: 978-1-925536-67-6

A note on differences in punctuation and spelling

Pure Slush Books proudly features writers from all over the English-speaking world. Some speak and write English as their first language, while for others, it's their second or third or even fourth language. Naturally, across all versions of English, there are differences in punctuation and spelling, and even in meaning. These differences are reflected in the work *Pure Slush Books* publishes, and they account for any differences in punctuation, spelling and meaning found within these pages.

Pure Slush Books is a member of the
Bequem Publishing collective
http://www.bequempublishing.com/

Alex Reece ABBOTT • Gary BECK • Paul
BECKMAN • Hakeem BEEDAR • Duncan BERCE
• Michael BERTON • Howard BROWN • Elizabeth
BUTTIMER • Robert CARLTON • Steven CARR •
Guilie CASTILLO ORIARD • Jan CHRONISTER
• Robert COOPERMAN • Carolyn CORDON •
Mark CRIMMINS • Judah Eli CRICELLI • Tony
DALY • Salvatore DiFALCO • Michael
ESTABROOK • Tom FEGAN • Nod GHOSH •
Geralda GJOMAKAJ • Ken GOSSE • Andrew
GRENFELL • Shane GUTHRIE • Robin HILLARD
• Jo HOCKING • Louise HOFMEISTER • Sharron
HOUGH • Mark HUDSON • Christine JOHNSON
• Jemshed KHAN • Michaeleen KELLY • John
LAMBREMONT Sr. • Jenny LAPEKAS • Ron.
LAVALETTE • Larry LEFKOWITZ • Peter
LINGARD • JP LUNDSTROM • Jenean
McBREARTY • Janet McCANN • Karla Linn
MERRIFIELD • David MILLER • Marsha
MITTMAN • Colleen MOYNE • Piet
NIEUWLAND • Emily O'SULLIVAN • Carl 'Papa'
PALMER • Melisa QUIGLEY • Charles
RAMMELKAMP • Lisa RHODES-RYABCHICH •
Ruth Sabath ROSENTHAL • Ed RUZICKA •
Shawn Aveningo SANDERS • Jeff SANTOSUOSSO
• Wayne SCHEER • Tom SHEEHAN • Lisa STICE
• Lucy TYRRELL • Vivian WAGNER • Alan
WALOWITZ • Mbeke WASEME • Michael WEBB •
Jeffrey WEISMAN • Debbie WIESS • Sharon
WILLDIN • George YATCHISIN

Contents

Poetry

Poetry

Lazy

Shawn Aveningo Sanders

Not your typical four-letter word
but it was the word I feared most—

Hearing it. Being labeled by it.
Inherent accusation *I wasn't worthy*.

And yes,
I grew up in the Midwest.

Hard work is a badge of honor.
Exhaustion, the reward.

That, and the company of fellow Missourians
or should I say misery-ans.

Show-me. Show-me.

If I show you my calloused hands
blisters, my achy-breaky back,

will that make you proud?
Will you show me your love?

Time's a wasting.
I have chores to finish.

The Slow Not

George Yatchisin

That dream with the sloth
at the other end of the seesaw.
How slowly nothing happened.
With its clever toes it won't
roll to you, gravity a kind
of impolite question. Let's say
you were grounded, and that
is what you wanted with the wild
so in touch, so out of reach.

Sitting with My Feet on a Pumpkin

Michael Estabrook

Indian summer
removed the fallen leaves
from the front gutter;
patched & painted
a leaking corner;
raked the lawn
& swept the steps
to the back deck;

now I'm sitting
with my bare feet propped up
on a big Halloween pumpkin,
listening to "Carmen",
my Mozart T-shirt on
nervous as usual
when things
are going well.

Loathing

Emily O'Sullivan

They think I'm lazy,
They think I'm idle,
I'm not.
I'm working.

They think I'm slow,
They think I'm slack,
I'm not.
I'm moving.

They think I'm apathetic,
They think I'm affectless,
I'm not.
I'm listening.

They think I'm careless,
They think I'm useless,
I'm not.
I'm trying.

They think I'm lethargic,
They think I'm indolent,
I am.
I'm dying.

Sloth am I

Tony Daly

Slumped on the street corner she begs
But too much work to extricate my wallet
So I walk on by with only a twinge of guilt
Sloth am I, for I neglect your plight for my comfort.

Slumped on the couch, eyes glazed
But too much work to hit the power button
So I sit, ignore life, and do not read to you
Sloth am I, for I neglect your education for my comfort.

Slumped on the floor, whining for food
But too much work it is to toss you a bone
So I eat and yell for you to be quiet
Sloth am I, for I neglect your health for my comfort.

Slumped in a hospital bed, awakening from a diabetic coma
But too much work it is to change my vices,
So I suck on the candy and go into shock,
Sloth am I, for I neglect myself for my own comfort.

Conservation of Energy

Ron. Lavalette

I meant to start mopping up
the last of that spilled and
spoiled milk a month ago
last week. I meant to start,
at least, to scrub those fugly
upstairs bathroom tiles
and—while I was at it—maybe
try to unclog the toilet or
open up one of the windows,
let in a breath or two of that
less fetid outside air.
I meant to. I really did.

I know I made a pledge
on New Year's Eve, a pledge
to change my ways, a pledge
to do the things that anyone
else—anyone with gumption—
would do in a heartbeat, do
without a second's thought;
but that was then, and this is
now. I'll get to it later. Maybe.

The way I see it's like this:
parked here on the couch,
I'm saving a bundle of cash
at the hardware store and the
laundromat; I'm not likely to
injure myself or wear out all
my shoe leather waiting for
take-out I don't have to cook.

Depressed Weight

Shane Guthrie

Faucet dripping water on unwashed dishes
I've tried turning it tightly
It drips anyway
I could fix it
Probably

It is too hard to rise
And every day it gets
Harder

The ceiling has a crack running through it
Maybe I could plaster it
Maybe the house is cracking in half
And the ceiling will open up
And fall on me
Kill me
That
Would
Be
Nice

Sloth in Texas

Janet McCann

Sitting in the abandoned
front garden, dogs investigating
the underbrush for possible
rats. The jasmine has
crawled across the pebbled walk
and the privet is grappling the eaves.
I think, listening to cars sigh past
this August morning, if I clipped,
if I cut back the branches and
peeled away the jasmine from the
stucco, if I planted pansies and
marigolds and heirloom roses,
then could I write? If I could only
clip away the berries on black
branches and the yellow nameless
star-like flowers that have invaded
from the unmowed yard? If I
replaced them with growing things
I knew by name, freesias, peonies,
then would I have order?
Then could I write?

The Man on the Porch

Howard Brown

Picture a man,
if you will, sitting
at high noon on
the porch of a
ramshackle house,
a structure in
such advanced
decay it seems
poised to implode.

A faint smile creases
his unshaved face;
otherwise he is
motionless and silent,
his gaze distant and
without focus, evincing
no sign he is aware of
his scolding wife, or the
gaggle of children who
boil about his weed-
choked yard.

Tell me, has he found
nirvana, or simply fallen
prey to the sin of sloth?

Summer Morning

Ed Ruzicka

We don't get many mornings this soft.
It is August and there is nothing to do.
I have eaten, have drunk, traveled,
sweated, played, raced, wrenched,
prayed for almost seventy years.

I have raised children
that are almost ready
to raise children of their own
so that I can sometimes
know what it is to breathe
inside of a jewel.

The Art Store

Mark Hudson

I recently entered a 12 by 12 art show in
my hometown at the local art store. First place
winner got a one hundred dollar certificate
for the store, two runners up got fifty dollar
certificates.

They said on the flyer, "Extra points
if your art piece contains a sloth, because
there is going to be a sloth there that night."

I thought that meant there would
be a man dressed up in a sloth costume,
which still sounded childish!

I went with my camera, but when
I got there, I realized the batteries on my
digital camera had just run out. So
tomorrow, I'll have to get batteries,
and I have no pictures of the show.

When I got there, it was all young
kids and their parents. And the staff
all look like teenagers. As a forty-seven-
year-old artist, I'm feeling old.

This man came up and introduced
himself. I've been seeing him at these
shows for years. But he never remembers
me. I guess I just have a good memory.
His picture had a sloth in it. I said,
"You might win." I think he came
in fourth or fifth place.

Then a man came in with a sloth,
a real-live zoo animal – a sloth! Here I
was thinking it would be a man dressed
as a sloth, but it was an animal – a sloth!
The sloth ate potatoes. The kids all
lined up to have their pictures taken
with the sloth.

I didn't win an award. There
was something very innocent about
the whole thing. They say it is a
family friendly store. I'm surprised
they let me in!

Sloth

Jemshed Khan

After lunch,
scurry out the kitchen door.

Close your eyes and climb
the backyard oak.

You know the route
by grip and foot and grunt.

Loll in the breeze
of the ample branch.

Catch the whiff of baking pie.
Hear dishes clink.

Slow your motion for hours
as the branches buzz and crawl

with six- and eight-legged curiosity.
Learn to dangle

by the crooks of your knees.
Soil your fingernails

and smudge your cheeks.
Dawdle if they call you in——

catch a cricket, chew a leaf.
But when Nana rings the bell,

rush inside to mashed potatoes
thick with gravy.

Lick the rhubarb
from your supper plate.

Then stretch your arms
and rest your head on the table.

When they ask for chores
yawn loudly once

and close your eyes
as if asleep.

Siesta \ Sleep as Ritual

Michael Berton

sleep when you are tired
of making the same old news
when you are undecided
on where to be heavy

sleep can make rest
play a little more at relaxation
sleep when you can't make
the day of your dreams

When the Cows Mosey on Home

Ruth Sabath Rosenthal

Father, what happens to cows when
they return home from the pasture at eventide?

Those that are steers earmarked "prime"
shall be slaughtered by & by.

But what of those big-bellied cows
that laze by the grassy wayside?

They'll express (albeit forced) utter
contrition — milk, the recompense they'll provide.

And what posture, in the big picture,
should diehard beefeaters take, and why?

For having consumed any part of that beast in the sub-
family *Bovinae* — in any way, shape, form, or size —

beefeaters, at apropos meals, should raise their glasses
in gratitude "for what we're about to eat," then apologize

(with all the humility they can gather) to all man-
ner of cows — domestic and worldwide!

Home Improvement

Jan Chronister

I can live with ill-fitting drawers
and doors. At least I know
where to find things. My poems
fly around the house
misguided insects
my sloth allows to settle
out of reach.

They ought to be caught
organized like silverware,
stacked in the pantry
like cans, as easy to find as food.

Onlooker

David Miller

Position – poolside
The first true
Gust of summer
Warm breeze encircling
Bunting fluttering
Papa Chango in the cans
Sprinting ducks
A public possibly
Unprepared
For my snowdrift skin
Best I remain seated
Catching glimpses
Of frolickers
With inflatables
Lap swimmers
Eyeing the clock
Concealed beneath
This shady tree
More a winter person now

On Line at
Border Control,
Charles DeGaulle Airport

Robert Cooperman

"The goddamn French love
their bureaucracy even more
than their baguettes and Brie,"
I fume to Beth, while we stand
on this airport line that will, in theory,
let us leave for home once we present
our passports at Border Control.
The line's more immobile than L.A.
rush-hour traffic backed up to San Diego.

Beth eases a calming hand on my shoulder,
and I tell myself, yes, this is typical
of the French—too slothful to man
Border Control when there are croissants
and good French coffee on their breaks
that last longer than our flight will—
but at least we're not fleeing a warzone,
only to be met by hatred and barbed wire.

The plane won't leave without us,
every passenger on it stuck in this line.
Or so I keep telling myself, while grinding
my teeth in rage, other passengers shouting
as if they're stranded in Casablanca,
Rick their one chance for safe passage
to neutral Portugal, while Paris Border agents
sigh and yawn, way too much trouble
and bother to actually stamp our passports.

Episodic Nothing

Jeff Santosuosso

Ball in flight,
dropped phone call,
imitation sweetener.

Who supplied my emotions?
They're on back order
or in transit.
I paid extra for handling.
My own, that is.

The ghost will not reveal itself.
It is not even dead.
Cloud-covered spirits stuck in the stratosphere,
they ride a rail of sunlight
100 billion miles, but can't make
the last two.

Somewhere, incomplete photosynthesis,
a leaf closes like a song

T-shirt

Lucy Tyrrell

Printed ink on fabric—
image of shaggy-haired mammal,
endearing beady eyes,
black button
nose on mask-like face.
Such a peculiar creature
hangs from limb by long
curved toenails,
three on each front foot,
not doing much more
than holding on.

Hard to discern inactivity—
or sluggish steps—
from simple outline, design
of sloth on shirt,
but the message is easily retained
even as the wearer walks away—
Cutest of the Deadly Sins.

Supersloth

Michaeleen Kelly

Jeremy hadn't anticipated the perverse suckiness of sloth –
how it conned you into putting out little or nothing.
Others will eventually pick up your slack
along with your discarded socks and everyday detritus
collecting in unlimited nooks
or in the underbellies of bedsteads, couches and coffee tables.

He imagined the architecture he was creating
with all the stashed and stacked stuff
revealed his unique, postmodern bricolage.
A towering testimony to his courage
in facing the void of absolute apathy.
His successful nighttime navigation
of the obstacle courses clear proof
of his Olympic-level hoarding competence.

Until the day he realized only indolent slum landlords
responding to reports of overwhelming stench and fire hazards
would witness his supersloth status.
Jeremy would be prepared for self-defensive strategies.
He had a lifetime of energy
stored up in the interstices of his slothful soul for such occasions.
The only setback?
Locating his home security system
that Rawlings baseball bat –
the one he hasn't seen since fifth grade.

Memory: South America

Marsha Mittman

Two children, ages five and seven
Skipping ahead of their parents
On a street in Caracas, Venezuela
Suddenly come to a halt

Turning, gesticulating wildly
Their faces full of joy and wonder
They point to some dark clump
Hanging from an exotic tree

At a distance we think
It's a large coconut or melon
But catching up we spy
Lazing away in the sunshine

A sloth

We lunch at an adjacent cafe
Yet even strategically thrown
Tidbits don't entice the indolent
Creature to join the party

Weeks later at home I overhear
A repeated taunt after chastising
My apathetic son for leaving
A mess of toys strewn all about

My daughter, delighted with
Her brother's rebuke, prances
Around chanting disdainfully
You're a sloth, you're a lazy sloth

Travel is so educational

Nine Teas

Lisa Stice

My grandma says no—
she does not want them,

and she was always a tough
one to stir, with little sugar,

just steeping on a bench
while we hurried through

malls, museums, record shops.
My grandma says no—

to drives through orchards
and walks around the home

because she always said no
and so why should we expect

after all this time of bittering
she would want to drink

life up or even watch a movie
from six teas ago that she was never

interested in before, and so
leaves fall and remain there.

Teen Manger

Louise Hofmeister

Can't clean my room,
I'm busy –
I'm making hormones here.

Don't bother me,
I'm in bed *cuz*
the clothes are on the chair.

Stop knocking! No, you
can't come in –
my piles are sorted there.

Say what, til clean
you've locked me in?
Is this some kind of zoo?

If you won't let me out
I'll starve,
What kind of parent are you?

It's Time

Colleen Moyne

I'm becoming concerned
about the thing
in the corner –

I think it's alive!
It didn't arrive,
didn't wander in;
it just... became

this shapeless creature
without a name

Sometime between
sleep and work
and work and sleep
it began to creep
across the floor

and sprawl
like a lazy cat
sunning itself
against the settee

But now
in a shaft of sunlight
from the window
I see

It's not a creature at all

It's jeans and jocks
and dirty socks
and yesterdays shirt

and soggy towels
and dirty sheets
and all manner of dress

piled up in a sloppy mess,

beginning to take on
a life of its own

morphing and growing,
feeding on sweat and grime...

I think it might be laundry time.

Finding the Sweet Spot

Elizabeth Buttimer

That man was born lazy, he's so lazy
if he were a hound dog he wouldn't
bother to swat flies with his tail,
he wouldn't lift his head even
a teensy bit if he saw his master
walking up to the front porch
he wouldn't even sniff if golden
brown hushpuppies cooked
in bacon grease bubbled on the stove
just waiting to find their way to his
bowl. If he were a hound dog
he wouldn't even thump his tail
at the chance to spark with a female
dog in season. Nope, he wouldn't
open his eyelids just a crack
if the wooden boards were swept
clean around where he lay or

if a snake, big as your leg, crawled
under the house into his dirt dug
cool spot under the wrap around.
There ain't nothing to make him
motivated, to make him sit up
and pay attention except
a woman, built like a lumberjack,
armed with a giant cast iron skillet
big as the moon and a swing
like the Babe headed for the back
of his head, now that makes him
move like greased lightning.

Blame?

Carolyn Cordon

Is there a line between
slothful and lazy?
And if there is,
is it fuzzy, hazy?
Does it start at OKish
then morph to the worst?
Is one ok, or are both
fatally cursed?

If I lie in bed, wrapped in sleep
slothful or lazy, which would it be?
Slowly moving, languid, serene
my blanket – leaves, my bed – a tree.
Or am I a hateful, lazy, no good person
hiding when I should be working
like others do, respectful, good –
while I'm always bad & lazily shirking?

Or do the two merge, forever blending
then separating again? I'm facing the truth
or trying to – working a bit as best I can –
but only sometimes, is that the proof
I'm lazy AND slothful, a human sloth
slacking off always, & should be shamed?
But we all love sloths, up in their trees
if I act like them, should I be blamed?

Digital Sloth

Karla Linn Merrifield

After I *untangle the beasts*
of distraction (e.g., Facebook friends,
poetry fans, even my husband)?
After I dismantle the demons
of idleness (1. afternoon naps,
2. gossipy emails, 3. Netflix
instant downloads 24/7)?
After the gnarly crap—
my doctors, lawyers, editors—
is whisk-broomed metaphorically away,
siphoned off into a black hole?
The rest is a trite piece 'o cake:

And the sonnet's final truth has something
to do with zebra-winged butterfly wings.

with a line from Chris Crittenden's 'Under the Silver'

Sloth Poem

Debbie Wiess

The call is out: pieces about Sloth are desired.
Certainly a grand subject by which to be inspired.
And most enticing the glories of success.
If one can overcome the fear, insecurity and stress.
But then the realization that more than a little work
may be required.
Thus in a creative morass I find myself mired.
So without further ado have I put down my pen,
yawned and retired.

Flight Jacket

Judah Eli Cricelli

Voices
That mean
Nothing to us,
The smell of
Fresh-cut grass
And dogshit.
A stain
On shirt:
Is it
Blood,
Or melted
Ice block?
Thoughts
And altered memories,
There was a kind of
Conclusiveness
To the air,
That wrapped up
All your
Loose ends.
We move
Together,
Working through
The nightmare,

Finding meaning
In something
Meaningless
And soon
We become
Able to hear
Insecurity
In other people's voices,
Surrounded by
Relics
Of an
Inert time.
Memory
Is a
Warm wind
On a cold day
That makes
Your stomach
Shudder,
It is
A voice
That means
Nothing to us,
An eye
Inside
A
Coffee cup.

I lean against
The counter,
Waiting for the kettle
To boil,
And for the
First time in my
Adult life,
I almost
Feel like
Some kind of
Grown-ass man,
A problem
I will
Go on
To do nothing
To change.
Voices
That mean
Nothing to us:
And we never stop
To ask each other
If this
Is all
We want
To hear.

Invitation for Coffee

Carl 'Papa' Palmer

You'll just have to excuse my dirty house
does not prepare us as she moves an arm-
load of clutter from the food-stained couch.

Waiting for us to sit are several large cats
purring intentions of sharing laps and fur
as four or five more meow into the room.

I hope you both like instant while wiping
room on her coffee table for three wet cups,
a dusty plastic plate of garlic pretzel mix,

four grey sugar cubes on a Subway napkin,
and half full quart of fat free milk showing
blue through the month old expiration date.

We rise in unison, brush hair from our slacks,
and reach for our coats almost before we hear
her exclaim, *I can't believe I'm out of coffee.*

The Slothful Landlord

Lisa Rhodes-Ryabchich

I see her for the first time,
a conniving evil woman, hell bent
on ruining our vacation.
A lying self-deprecating miniature Hitler,
carefully constructing chaos: the dirt

in the corners, obviously untouched,
black hairs on the bathroom floor,
were embedded
in the rotting legs of the vanity,
black beetles casually crawled from behind
the toilet & in the living room,

dishes were left cluttered
in the dish drying rack
& still wet when we first arrived,
& the refrigerator bin was smeared
with mayonnaise.

The previous tenant, left bags
of organic peas, stacked in the freezer,
& a myriad of strange, used condiments, hung
on the door.
The internet service, never connected,
until three magical days, before
we had to go home.

Dingy sheets were left sloppily stacked
on top of the beds, & the issue of
the slight red stain,
in the seam, of the middle couch pillow cover,
& barely visible, & her insistence that we buy

a brand-new couch. The teasing painting
of beach waves like white curling rope, hung
over the kitchen doorway aiming to create,
a normal environment. Above the fireplace,

in the living room, a "Welcome to Paradise" sign,
hung unobtrusively.
One day, I noticed a trumpet flower vine, gracefully
bobbing in the window, by the kitchen sink.

The rain had spattered on it, in the evening
so it was lush & illustrious, like an opera singer—
the only thing that remained viable, good & sweet,
promising a healing—a life that would continue

to erase, the negativity of this landlord: her poison
entrails insisting we go home early
in her threatening emails, & voice messages.
The vodka bottle, found chilling in the freezer—
ready to explode—still patiently awaited.

Sloth

Geralda Gjomakaj

This morning is the first day of my life,
why do I stink of hubris already
in limbo of asleep and consciousness,
my positivity is shaky and my esophagus is breaking
my white sheets are clean
and the carpet beneath my feet quite pristine
I feel guilty of the incongruence,
My intestines feel infested, sooner or later
my insides will be projected
All over the walls, blackened with smoke,
floor filled with buds, books and sprinkles of coke
I feel heavy although I've lost a few pounds,
I'll feed off some more sleep before sundown
But my mind won't let me indulge in nothingness no more,
here comes the perpetual cycle
In which I trap myself in a thought loop,
psychology, philosophy, sociology word soup

I'm paralyzed as I become a spectator of the drama,
a wise interconnectedness of life's saga
Eventually my mind travels at a speed I lose track,
I feel I'll be left blind, deaf or amnesiac
Before I can recollect the bits of my consciousness
into cohesion and gain some prophetic vision,
as always, ice water and a smack await the other side
'Perhaps it's time you do something with yourself,' she says.

Sloth Au L'Overture

(an acrostic)

John Lambremont, Sr.

Tragic avoidance of activity,
Harming the prospect of proclivity,
Except as pertaining to work apathy.

Man by his nature's not a lazy beast;
Only by trying does he do his least;
Trees harbor sloths that he does imitate,
Helping his total worth to dissipate;
Ever will sloth truly be the queen mother,
Rendering more vices than any other.

Over and over from tasks turn away,
Finding they're still there the very next day;

Allow no visitors, shun inquisition;
Lay back at rest in a reclined position,
Let no one disturb your cherished non-mission.

Vagaries leave as new certainties grow;
Idiosyncrasies show from below;
Collect your thoughts, but don't put them to use;
Even to think seems a form of abuse;
Steady yourself with the next new excuse.

Flickering Ardor

Gary Beck

If we no longer care
for what once drove us
to passionate achievements,
we diminish ourselves
and become indifferent,
corrupt, nostalgic,
abandoning concern
with the state of the world.

Sinecure

Alan Walowitz

Better not to swallow
the time you need to kill—
it could eat you from within,
when make-work is readily available
to quell the incessant ticking in your head,
while waiting for the message
in your coffee cup to clear:
Your time is nearly up,—
yet you swallow as if it were the law.

Walk proud, purposeful and smart,
evading those who'll never appreciate the art
of bearing a single page one desk to next;
Post one more busy look— now
quizzical brow, puckered nose;
then, teeth gritted and grinding;
bend low to the task of tying your shoe—
you might decide to stay so long
the blood will rush from your head
like a highway.

Thank God there's lunch.
Though each bite makes us more bitter and insane,
it might feed us just enough
so we're ready to hit it running again,
posing as possessed, but in truth,
sans care, sans pride, sans everything;
meantime, some unheard voice
reminds us what must get done,
if there were only anything
worthy of all this doing.

Epitaffy for a
Mr. R. Van Winkle

Ken Gosse

They married quite young
but this beau was a catch:
from the town where they sprung,
'twas the best of the batch.

She cooked, cleaned, and sewed
but he did "all the rest."
Claims he carried the load,
although only in jest.

He gave her fine babies
but she gave them birth.
She soon learned his maybes
cost more than they're worth.

He promised her all,
sun and moon, stars and sky,
but ne'er found his "call"
as the years drifted by.

It's not that he's lazy
or never would try,
but his plans were all hazy—
or simply a lie.

She pinched every penny
she managed to earn.
He never earned any,
but used them in turn.

She hung on for many
long years in his dust.
He never did any—
thing that she could trust

which would bring home the bacon,
pay bills, offer fun,
and this left her heart achin'
to try a new run

for a new lease on life
with a man who's a man,
who would care for his wife
just like Adam began.

Then her forehead of wrinkles
sent hope to her heart;
and here's where Van Winkle's
long story would start.

She packed him an herb
which would cause a deep sleep
from which none could disturb,
though his body would keep.

They found him that eve,
just as dead as a beast.
Time to mourn and to grieve,
so they called for a priest.

Rip's dream is a story
we all know by rote.
A legend from Irving,
but truth? Not a mote.

And what of the widow?
A tiger, perhaps?
Nightmarish libido
for men who take naps?

He pledged her his troth
and though he did his best,
his tombstone read "Sloth"
when she laid him to rest.

Good Neighbors

Vivian Wagner

The dead
rest quietly
this morning
across the street
from my house.
They demand nothing,
need nothing,
have no bills to pay.
The sun warms
them as they
keep the trees and
grass company,
and the mourning doves
cooing above
only sound sad.

Bougainvillea Boulevard

Piet Nieuwland

In the city of lost alphabets
With women who explode from flowers by Givenchy and
Versace
At the pool on Bougainvillea Boulevard
Surrounded by laden orange trees and a bamboo hedge
Summer melts from the midday sky, the water a very
comfortable 28 degrees C,
Salty clear fresh, the city google maps itself into endless distant
ripples
It feels like we are on our own here but that sense quickly dispels
A helicopter and Lear jet pass over and cars
Race down Balboa on the third and final week of our laziness
There are signs of inattention and decay, rust on the pool step,
cracks in the mosaic tiles, tears in the deck chair cloth, trees
with pale yellow leaves, bare broken branches, a mechanical
fault in the pump and pipes, the fountain issuing from a bronze
mermaid with dolphins is intermittent and we resign ourselves
to its destiny
Move on to enjoying another relaxed lunch of brie with Le
Pain Quotidien bread of the day, cherries, grapes, Perrier
sparkling lime water, perhaps a glass or two of brut

The rose makes easy lengths of the pool as a humming bird
vanishes through the hedge
In a small nearby pool oversized carp gently disco in the silvery
light below a mossy waterfall
A breeze washes through the bamboo again drawn by an event
of operational significance for someone, not our problem.
But the sound of raised voices, Spanish, from an apartment
nearby, a dog barks, perhaps a Chihuahua or terrier, high
without depth or resonance, somehow a fine mist leaks from
the blue, an almost invisible rain of scented droplets,...

A Day in the Life of a Smoker

Tom Sheehan

He turned on the coffeepot; when it was ready poured himself a cup. The pack of Camel smokes seemed to materialize from nowhere. It was more of rote, he realized, but he neither drank nor had a smoke while waiting for the paper to come, third element of his morning ritual. Coffee aroma, heavy and nostalgic about him. The sun placed its hands across the kitchen table. It could be perfect, he thought, but the pain came back as it had for a long, long time.

Out the kitchen window he looked, down gentle slopes and over solid geometry of rooftops and lawns and pools, parts of the Oaklandvale section of Saugus, a blacker crow's ten miles north of Boston; just go over the Tobin Bridge looking up toward Maine. Once, this had been perfect. Casey had been perfection. Life had been different. One time he never coughed for a whole day.

When the thud came at the front door, he retrieved the *Globe*, sipped his coffee, lit a Camel from the pack of cigarettes. At the second drag of a Camel he coughed, gagged, caught phlegm in his mouth and spit noisily in the hopper of the downstairs bathroom.

His wife Elaine spoke from the head of the stairs. "If you had stopped smoking, Bob, you really wouldn't sound so disgusting in the morning." A hopelessness trailed away with her voice, like a far road she had been down too many times.

Cocoon

Melisa Quigley

Slow to move
affronted by life
expected to marry
not wanting a wife
slurping on fizzy drinks
and playing game boy
thirty-five years old
always wanting
more new toys
eating pizza
not wanting to cook
clothes unchanged
bursting at seams
hair not washed
couldn't care less
empty pizza boxes line the floor
Bling! Bling!
another person dead
wanting to kill more

Prose

Prose

The Fitness

Andrew Grenfell

The guy is, what's the word? Pontificating. Mind you, I have sort of encouraged him.

"I like to do my workouts in the morning. The earlier the better, you know?"

I think about my own morning. When did I wake up? Sometime around 11, I think. And only because the sun was lancing into the room by then, baking me starfished on my futon.

"Yeah," I say, trying to muster some interest. The citadel of my wine glass stands emptily on the snow white landscape of the tablecloth. "High motivation levels in the morning."

The guy is oblivious to sarcasm. I dimly remember he's in banking, must be a colleague of the groom. He has impressively carved shoulders.

I look properly into his eyes, their clear crystal blue.

The hubbub of the reception falls away as I let my mind slide into imagining being enfolded in his steel-strong arms. My eyes close with exceptional bliss. He breathes in my freshly washed hair and the array of scents I have anointed myself with according to my highly regular beauty routine.

"I'm always starting on the treadmill. Gotta have a decent warm up, feel like you're going somewhere."

"Mmmmm."

After I dragged myself out of bed I scanned through memes and dumb videos on the Internet for, maybe, two hours. There was a funny one about a bodybuilder and a protein shake.

"Then I'm bumping reps." He makes a punching fist motion thing. I suppose he's trying to emanate infectious enthusiasm. I can't get a look at his pecs, but I'm sure they ripple like sand on the ocean floor.

We've had two or even three perfectly healthy babies and we work hard at jobs with very prescribed hours that nevertheless fulfil us professionally. We renew our annual gym memberships at the same time and experiment with different pulverised fruit drinks. Evenings are spent planning elaborate dinner parties and learning a foreign language together. On Fridays we have athletic, even exhausting sex.

"No-one ever regretted going to the gym," I agree. I try to catch the eye of the roving wait staff – they were refilling reliably half an hour ago, so what happened?

"It's a funny thing, isn't it, that you can feel energised from exercise."

"I reckon!" I had dragged myself to the shower once I suddenly realised I had under an hour to get ready and get to the ceremony, and I wasn't exactly smelling acceptable. There followed a confusing whirlwind of thrown clothes around the bedroom punctuated with a good deal of swearing.

The bride and groom are about to start off the wedding waltz. This man is going to ask me to dance, because we're the only two singles at the table, and I'm 99% sure we were sat next to each other for that reason. The planes of his chin make me think of smooth white ocean liners.

I enthusiastically support his triathlons on the weekend, clapping like a mad person. On long drives we patiently explain important concepts to our growing curious children, smiling wryly to each other at their naïve questions. The garden is manicured to within an inch of its life. We have one dog, and one cat, which are well behaved because we have put the time in to train them, unlike some other pet owners we could name.

The dessert – altogether too creamy and sugary, and altogether too much eaten – gurgles disturbingly in my stomach. I feel the creases in my dress, partly bunched up between my thighs and the chair. The music has kicked up a notch.

"Do you want to dance, then?" he asks.

Which is really the question, isn't it? Is there a version of me which doesn't catch even a blip of daytime TV, which leaves no toast crumbs on the couch, no shoes strewn on the floor, doesn't stay up later every night in a hazy blue glow, grazing absentmindedly through the pantry every twenty minutes?

"Nah," I say. "I'm good as is."

Dead End

Jenny Lapekas

I've always been a student. As a little girl, I sauntered around museums so that I could absorb everything as deeply and delicately as possible, while others scolded me to catch up. I was frequently reprimanded by my father when he checked on me during nap time, only to discover a pile of books underneath my quilt and my eyes shut a bit too tightly, feigning sleep. I'd happily forego sleep, miss a ride or pester someone if it meant that I could learn something interesting.

In eighth grade, I skipped math class to see a production of Edgar Allan Poe's short story 'Hop-Frog'. I lingered after the play ended, eager to immerse myself in this newfound subculture of creative people.

"You're aspiring," one of the actors said to me after we chatted for a bit.

When I asked him, "To what?" he shrugged and said he didn't know, implying that this part was up to me. The actor's words stayed with me long after that moment in my high school auditorium.

After studying English in college, I worked at a grocery store for about a year until I decided I could take no more rude customers and minimum wage paychecks. I thought I might be ready to make the transition from student to teacher, to share what I had learned from my late-night reading and expensive college classes.

Broke and disheartened, I suggested to my mother that I apply to graduate school, but the idea didn't sit well with her. She worked steady hours as an RN in a women's prison in New Jersey and a psychiatric hospital in Pennsylvania, earning enough money to install new floors in our old farm house and hop on flights to Poland, China and Africa whenever she pleased. With low pay, unlikely benefits and zero job security looming in her daughter's future, she tried her best to protect me.

"You'll never get a job," she scolded, standing over the dishwasher with a tired look of disapproval.

"I guess I'll just be a starving writer!" I countered, throwing my arms up in surrender, shaking off the wet blanket I had come to see her as.

She finally compromised by financing my degree if I agreed to study Secondary Education, rather than English. *Fine*, I told myself, *I'll teach composition and literature to high schoolers.* Ugh. I remember the teenage me: the arrogance, the sarcasm, the distorted sense of entitlement. Who did I think I was, anyway? I attended a small university for about a year, and I was miserable. I learned that I would be a role model as an educator, someone who students could look up to. *Me?* I thought. *The girl who laughs when people discuss fine art? The girl who eats an entire pack of Jaffa Cakes in ten minutes? The girl who cries at pictures of disabled cats on Pinterest?* My premature case of Impostor Syndrome was almost too much to bear.

I quickly grew bored with my classes. Some of my professors preferred to discuss Lady Gaga or the *Twilight Saga* over the reading we were assigned. The academic rigor I had come to expect was replaced by a lingering sloth and easy complacency that I could only assume had been established long before my arrival. My drama instructor wept openly in class meetings and discussed the intimate details of her early days in the theater. As the semester drew to a close, I was mildly surprised to find nothing about them on the final exam. After a semester and a half, I didn't feel challenged by my teachers or enthusiastic about my coursework. A future that involved teaching the literary canon to high schoolers also looked rather grim. I had to get busy aspiring.

I dreamed of reaping the benefits of *thinking*, not just sitting through classes that I quietly resented, daydreaming about napping with Huck Finn in the woods, cozying up to Grendel in his musty cavern, or attending Ray Bradbury's dark carnival. I wanted to board a train, talk to a mysterious stranger, eat the food of the spirits, soaking in the newfound revelation that stories help us to understand who we are, that words should be celebrated like a homecoming and exercised like a muscle, utilized to pluck at nerves, harness fears and uncover truths.

Unfortunately, my peers didn't share my concerns. I began to feel like the jester from 'Hop-Frog', a walking punchline about to spontaneously combust. Like the unfortunate dwarf, I was force-fed the wine and told that I should enjoy it, but I was secretly planning my escape. I needed more. Give me the grief of Dickinson, the earthy undercurrent of Whitman, the punchy lines of Hemingway. Let these voices marinate in my soul for a bit, and I'll find my way from there. What I wanted was a graduate degree in English. After that, who knows? The *who knows?* element that I found so thrilling was what terrified my mother.

I decided to commit to a different path, a more romantic one that perhaps wouldn't lead to a career in writing, but to authentic learning and self-discovery. I handed in my student ID, officially withdrew from my classes and breathed a sigh of relief. As I walked triumphantly back to my car, my footsteps the only sound on a deserted stretch of sidewalk, I wondered which direction led out of the mishmash of alleys, side streets and parking lots. I must have looked like a bright-eyed freshman as I peered out my car window at street names and other signs. DO NOT ENTER. *Okay, maybe this way, back toward the fitness center.* YIELD. *Yeah, I'm just gonna pull a U-turn and head in this direction.* I switched off the chatter on the radio and shielded my eyes from the glittering sun, staring at yet another sign: DEAD END. I couldn't help but laugh as I rolled to a stop, turned around and kept going.

Lazybones

Charles Rammelkamp

"Enjoy your well-deserved rest," the card had read at Philip Strohminger's retirement luncheon. More than a dozen of his colleagues had signed it. The message sounded as if he had died. *Well-deserved rest?*

Indeed, most of Strohminger's co-workers at the agency seemed baffled that he would retire at the age of sixty-two, as if it were a copout, a shirking of responsibilities.

Six months later, when he met Harry O'Sullivan for lunch, "What are you going to do?" had morphed into "What do you do?"

"I don't know," Strohminger shrugged. Wasn't this the point of retirement? No longer keeping a status report going? He didn't particularly keep track. He could mumble about "the grandkids" or mention his wife Linda, but the question meant more than that. *How do you justify your existence?* He had his pastimes to be sure – wrote poems, edited a small online poetry journal, corresponded with other writers, read books. But what had he been *doing* before he retired?

"What about you, Harry? What do you do?"

"What do you mean, what do I do?" O'Sullivan replied, astonished he was even being asked. "I'm up to my ears in agency projects, the time-and-attendance logs, the earnings-and-benefits reports, the employee technical progress chronicles." He waved his arms to suggest the myriad things he was *doing*.

"But do you still read the newspaper with your bagel and coffee in the morning, shoot the shit with Bernie and Bob and the rest at the weekly pinochle game in the fourth floor lounge?"

"Ha ha," O'Sullivan said. "What do you do besides collect the pension check and the Social Security you filed for at sixty-two rather than wait until you're sixty-five and get a bigger check? Watch soap operas? Game shows? Jerry Springer?"

"Nope, no soaps, no Springer."

"But what do you *do*?"

"What does anybody *do*? Eat, sleep, pay bills. Read, write."

"Oh, that's right. You're a poet, an *artiste*." The sarcasm made Strohminger blush, not that he hadn't heard this before. It was why he never brought it up with O'Sullivan and his oh-so-important time-and-attendance work.

Phil Strohminger shrugged elaborately then in an *OK-you've-got-the-goods-on-me* gesture. "All right," he conceded, "I admit it. I'm a lazy, good-for-nothing slothful parasite sucking on the government's tit, one of Mitt Romney's forty-seven percent. I'm a deadly sinner, and sloth is my poison! Okay?"

Now it was O'Sullivan's turn to be embarrassed. "Oh, it's OK, Phil," he soothed, all at once magnanimous. "I'm just raggin' you. But if you want to come back to the agency part-time, I'll put in a good word for you."

I'd rather slit my wrists, Phil Strohminger thought, but he just smiled and shrugged.

All Happy Families

Salvatore DiFalco

Fredo took out a bowl to prepare the tuna. It was almost noon. He felt blocked up. He'd been feeling very blocked up of late. The weather wasn't helping, recent cyclones and so on. The world had changed so much in such a short time. He stared at his hands: they were the blue of Uranus. His neighbour, Luke, had once showed him a picture of Uranus in an astronomical book. Luke died last year. One day he told Fredo he was dying of pancreatic cancer. Two weeks later he was dead. The tuna smelled a little off. But tuna always smells a little off, Fredo concluded. You probably wouldn't want to eat it if it smelled like custard or apple pie. He chopped an onion and a cucumber. Using a discarded toothbrush, he mixed these in with the tuna. He ground in black pepper. The pepper mill, a sturdy metal and glass tube, had belonged to an old man who used to live around the corner. On the very day he died, the very moment, Fredo happened by his house and heard him groaning. He charged inside, announcing he was a First-Aider, but the old man had expired. The pepper mill was a memento of the incident. Fredo felt no guilt about taking it. He ground extra pepper into the mix. Then he chopped up two fat earthworms he had plucked out of the garden that morning. The worm bits continued writhing as he mixed them with the tuna, onion and cucumber. Grandpa insisted on Miracle Whip in his tuna sandwiches. One time, years ago, when Fredo, in a moment of distraction, had used mayonnaise, Grandpa made him kneel on popcorn kernels until he passed out from the pain. "Fredo!" Grandpa shouted. "Fredo!" He had the most annoying voice in the universe. He sounded like a big dog with throat cancer. He couldn't walk anymore. Or he didn't want to walk anymore. It was a toss up. He weighed 400 pounds and spent most of his days and nights trussed up on the California king bed in his bedroom. When Fredo brought up the sandwich, he had to loosen the straps holding Grandpa's thighs apart. It took some doing. Grandpa smelled bad, like a rotting animal. "Go on," he cackled, "loosen me up." Then he wanted Fredo to apply lotion to his badly chafed calf muscles. "Now?" he said. "Now," said Grandpa. Fredo slathered medicated lotion over his thick, pimply calf muscles. While he worked, Grandpa swatted him with a gift-wrapping tube. It made a hollow thumping music when it struck his head. "You're useless, Fredo. Useless." Thump. "Look at you, still in your pajamas." Thump thump. "What 40-year-old man spends his days in pajamas?" Thump. Fredo held his tongue. You can't hate someone for being a bitter fat old man. Well, you can. But what can you do about it? The past is the past. You have to move forward. Fredo looked at his hands: still as blue as Uranus. Funniest thing. They weren't numb or anything. Just that peculiar hue of blue. Life is full of mysteries. Grandpa grabbed the sandwich and started eating.

My Day Off

Duncan Berce

I don't have to be at work today. None of my friends or family are offering or pressuring to socialise. Yesterday I took the dog for a walk, did some push-ups and sit-ups in my bedroom and ate well. I am not hungover, and I have been a little bit of a socialite all week. All ingredients have been added for fertilising the ultimate day off.

My equilibrium rotates in a warmly liquid lucidity, rocking gently back and forth and stretching out with the mild ease of a foetus in the womb. My toes spread and curl, pulling the muscles and tendons beneath the soles of my feet into a satisfying, near-cramping stretch. As the post-midday sun swings idly across the doming blue sky, the wispy golden sunlight flooding down is broken into shade by the leaves of the swaying eucalyptus tree above me. The tickle of vitamin D rides down the rope of the hammock on which I hang, breathing into the skin of my feet and up through my legs into the rest of my body. An exquisite ripple of pleasure warms my yawning face and my stretching arms crack at the elbows, my fingers brushing the pale smooth bark of the branch to which my hammock is attached.

I feel quite like a sloth, dangling on the branch of some ancient rainforest tree, dopey smile smeared onto my face that sags with the contentment of continuous lazy yawning. The thick hooks of his fingers are like the ropes and his warm, shaggy fur is like the soft woven cotton of my hammock. The world passes by and he and I suddenly share a kindred appreciation for just stopping still, making oneself comfortable and allowing the mind to flow out into the insatiable threading of thought. I kind of feel bad for the Sloth, I mean, he has been named as one of the Seven Deadly Sins. For God's sake, why is the poor guy considered sinful? Take a good look at his smiling face as he slowly regards your passing and tell me he is not just enjoying being alive? As I feel now, I can understand his method of being, because it is as un-impactful as it is un-intrusive, he just does his own thing. If the Sloth understands that peace and happiness in life is achieved through just enjoying being here, I think the Sloth may be tapped into a more enlightened and empowered wavelength than most "intelligent" humans. If being a Sloth is considered a sin, I think maybe it cannot be because he is regarded as a symbol for laziness, because that just seems like a very blatant misrepresentation. Maybe it is sinful to be like the Sloth because what he represents is the mindset of an individual, an individual that needs nothing else in life to provide it with meaning or purpose and so cannot be manipulated. I can see how this idea could be overtly threatening to an organisation that demands strict conformity via manipulation through commandments and if to sin is to break these commandments and the commandments disavow individuality, then the system is protected. Poor guy, the Sloth; the world's most loveable scapegoat.

I squeeze my eyes shut, my vision of the leaves and sky above cut off but still bright red as the sun's rays gently try to pry my soft lids open. I am now at the mercy of my other senses, every sound, smell and sensation riding out on the currents they know and brushing back into my mind to paint a picture of my own little snow-globe. A far-off plane breaks through the quiet dome like distant thunder, falling across the dim hubbub of muted traffic resting just above the trees and rooftops. Something tickles at my left forearm and I give it an absent-minded scratch, shuffling my leg into a bend. I had to mow the lawns yesterday and the dewy tang of cut grass remains, bitter in my nostrils but also pleasantly sweet.

I hear a little Bee swerve by, rather too close for my mental defensive measures. My mind aims in the direction of the potential threat, but I feel my currently motionless search for whatever it is human beings search for is not impeding the little fellow on his journey to discover new flowers swollen with pollen. I am but a passing oddity and so despite the warning signs flashing red, I am not particularly worried. How often it is that I watch other people go by, like this little Bee, off on their own adventure, with their own deep fears, joys, loves, flaws and virtues and wonder who they are, who they impact with their circle of existence and how the world will be changed by their being alive. I see all animals like that. Sloths, Bees, Humans; when my mind goes off like this, it is a kind of yearning out into the infinite void about the existence of life after my own death and something I cannot ever know.

I open my eyes because if my other senses are left to guide my over-active mind, I am prone to analysing philosophical circles. If there is one thing in this life I cannot stand it is pointless philosophy. Metaphorical mind traps that make one question everything annoy me because there are so many questions to find answers for, why waste time with the answerless ones? I sigh and close my eyes again. You really need to try and enjoy doing nothing, nothing but exist and listen to the world. You really need to enjoy your days off.

First World Dilemma

Sharon Willdin

11am Sunday

Busted with my finger in the peanut butter jar and ripping a baguette apart with my teeth.

"Thought you were dieting," snooted Sara as she emerged from the bedroom catching me red-handed.

"After this," I muffled with a mouth stuffed full of bread.

She flicked her hair extensions behind her as she picked up a tabloid magazine from the coffee table. Her loose-fitting joggers outlined a perfectly taut bum which she'd achieved from the weighted squats she did daily at the gym.

"Well I hope you washed your hands. You're not the only one in this house who likes to eat you know."

She strutted to the fridge, prudently selected a bowl of grapes and returned to the bedroom.

12pm Sunday

Kicked my feet up in front of the TV, accompanied by the last slice of a baked cheesecake.

Sara materialised like an obsessed stalker. "Thought you said you were on a diet."

Shocked by her sudden appearance, I swallowed a spoonful of cheesecake down the wrong way and coughed. "Just finishing this first."

Her fixed stare, bloated lips, and false eyelashes resembled an emu the moment before it attacks.

Instead she spat, "The key is willpower, you know."

She marched to the kitchen, smoothed a wedge of avocado over a rice cracker and returned to the bedroom to continue her microscopic examination of the world's most beautiful people.

1pm Sunday

Grabbed a packet of salted caramel pretzels from the pantry and a cold beer from the fridge.

Snuck to the lounge, took a swig of beer but kept a cautious eye on the bedroom door. Thought I'd made it. But there she was. Hands on hips, blocking my view of the football.

"A new type of diet, no doubt?"

I repressed a burp and held up my beer. "Low carb."

The injections they'd put in her forehead didn't allow her to frown but I could tell she was angry from the lump that bulged like an inverted horn above her nose. Exasperated by my lack of self-discipline, she stormed off.

2pm Sunday

Rang for a pizza, double cheesy garlic bread and an oozy chocolate lava cake.

She poked her head out. Watched me make the phone call. No protest. She just retreated into her cave.

Thirty-six minutes later the door-bell buzzed. I tipped the delivery driver, put my feet up, slapped open the box, began to salivate, and was just about to take a bite when I heard the creak of the bedroom door.

"What's this then?" she half-scolded but lacked any actual conviction.

"Starting tomorrow."

"Great. I'm starving!" She plunked down next to me and dug in. Scoffed everything.

After she finished she snuggled into my shoulder like a content kitten resting on a padded pillow. "Love you babe. So glad you appreciate me for who I really am," she purred.

"Same."

Becoming a sloth not so easy

Jeffrey Weisman

Two- and three-toed sloths have it easy. They enter the world as sloths and do what sloths do. Virtually nothing.

Humans have to learn to become sloths. They need to practice…or, actually not practice.

Sloths sleep some 15 hours a day. I sleep 10 hours per night plus a daily two-hour nap. Only three hours to go. I need more practice sleeping.

Upon awakening, I reheat yesterday's coffee and sit down at the computer. Some years ago, I deleted most of my email feeds. Yet I will sit watching the screen waiting for an email to show up. I also waste time reading the never-ending Facebook time line. This makes me a media sloth.

During my business career, inertia kept me moving. The day's activities carried over into the evening and weekends too.

Now, inertia keeps me at rest. I've stopped wearing a watch. Often I'll skip lunch. Too much effort to prepare it. Or maybe I'll eat a can of soup right out of the can, undiluted, unheated. The ingredients remain the same, after all.

Why call Sloth a Deadly Sin? What's the real problem with idleness or indolence? Sloth hurts no one. Sloths do not take up space that others could occupy.

Rather, doing nothing makes sense to me now. I'm taking a vacation from normality. Who cares if I sleep in my clothes? It saves time dressing the next day.

This should not imply that I have become a slob. Far from it. I shower more or less every day. I keep myself fairly well groomed. How often does one really need to shave? I just don't do anything requiring more than a modest amount of energy.

A day in the life of a human sloth requires sitting, waiting for something to happen, thinking of the tasks one might do and then not doing them.

Two- and three-toed sloths hang upside down from tree branches. I lie on my back on a two-person love seat, my hands and feet pointing up over the arm rests. In a sense I'm emulating my sloth cousins.

Often I'll just sit and stare. The only words that come into my mind spell what you just read: I just sit and stare. I may even concentrate on doing nothing, a step beyond meditation.

Sometimes, sitting in front of the television, I'll aimlessly watch whatever comes on – mesmerized, immobile, stupefied. I don't exert the energy to change the channel, even with the remote control close at hand.

As they age, people joke about walking into a room and not remembering why. I do that. A true sloth wouldn't even try to remember.

Society decries inactivity. In contrast, I find slothiness, doing nothing, quite satisfying.

After working some 40 years, one must relax. The "experts", sociologists and psychologists and do-gooders, claim that activity will keep you young. But you're already 70 or 75. How young can you become?

Rather, slowing down after running your whole life might make some sense. You always have the choice to begin to run again.

The way-too-busy world will tempt you. People will tell you not to waste your days. They won't come back. But doing nothing for a while couldn't hurt.

Before my nap, allow me to offer some advice: Try a little sloth for a change.

My Epiphany

Peter Lingard

It's taken until my umpty-umph year to reach a momentous epiphany. The experience can be likened to my schoolboy fear of the Pythagorean Theorem. It was supposedly difficult to grasp but, when presented, made immediate sense to me. Another example was the day (magnificent day) I experienced what I'd known only in theory: that kissing a girl was a prelude to ecstasy. Then there was the day a job recruiter believed that, having been a Marine, I was bound for employment in marine shipping. But the latest epiphany has brought me great joy. It's like having shackles taken off my feet. It's put a smile on my face, and caused me to experience the ridiculous sensation of wanting to chuckle. And it's so simple! My feet should never be identically clad. I have taken all the paired socks out of my sock drawer, unrolled them, paired them with delightfully different step-brothers and rerolled them. Now, when I wear a green sock on my left foot, I wear a blue one on my right ... or I might change them around. Does the word 'ambidextrous' also apply to feet? I am my own fashion icon; singular because, inexplicably, my wife derives no delight in my sartorial revelation. Aside from what she calls my abhorrent style, she says I'm too lazy to pair my socks when the laundry is done. She made a good point in saying there'd no longer be any angst whenever an odd sock disappears from the laundry. I pointed out that I had re-sorted my sock drawer but she said, 'that's a one-time effort because for all future washings you can put any two together.' 'Yes!' I said, 'that's the whole point; no more uniformity.' She then asked why the necessity to roll odd socks? I could just throw them in the drawer and pull out any two socks whenever the need arose. That, however, is contrary to my idea of how to maintain a sock drawer and would indubitably allow my wife to shift gears from lazy to slothful. But I shall persist. Like Churchill, I shall fight on the beaches, I shall fight on the landing grounds, I shall fight in the fields and in the streets, I shall fight in the hills; I shall never surrender the newfound sense of freedom for my cumbersome and yet now dashing trotters.

No Sweat

Wayne Scheer

I could have been a star athlete. My coaches said I had the build, the natural ability, the smarts. I have one flaw: I'm lazy.

I've been lazy most of my life and I'm doing just fine.

I remember when I tried out for my high school basketball team. I was six feet tall and fourteen, so what else was I to do? In pickup games I was pretty good, and the game was fun, so I agreed when Coach Jackson asked me to try out for the team.

"You look pretty good, son," he said and winked. "I bet the ladies think so, too."

That's all he needed to say, as cheerleaders in short skirts shook their pom poms in my head. But this kindly father figure, who seemed genuinely concerned about me and my still dormant love life, turned into Hitler with a whistle at practice the first day.

"Give me 50 push ups, girls, then we'll go to the track for some wind sprints. All you sissies can drop out now!"

So I turned and went home.

That's the way I operated until my sophomore year in high school. I grew two more inches over the summer and bulked up. Me and my buddies lifted weights every day during the summer. I know I said I was lazy, but this was different. We worked out in Andy Sabbatino's garage and his sister Angie watched us. She was only fifteen, but I'm telling you: she could have passed for eighteen.

When school started, we decided to try out for teams because the jocks get the babes. Some of my buddies went for wrestling, but rolling on a mat with a sweaty guy wasn't for me. I already knew that basketball was too much work, and I sure wasn't about to knock heads with football freaks, so I figured baseball was perfect. Baseball is a slow, thoughtful game and you get to sit down every half inning.

And I was pretty good. I played a lot of Little League as a kid, and I knew how to hit. While other kids swung with their arms and shoulders, I understood the power came from the thighs and mid-section. I knew how to shift my weight from my back foot to my front foot and swing from the hips. I worked out at first base because of my size and because I figured it was the easiest position to learn.

Anyway, despite my lack of a work ethic, I became a high school star and won a baseball scholarship to the University of Arizona. By the time I got there I was six four and weighed two hundred and five pounds. The University tested me and said I had excellent eye-hand coordination and bat speed, and because my vision was good, they claimed they could teach me to see the spin on the ball so I could tell in advance which way the ball would break.

With all this "natural talent" they predicted I would make varsity by my sophomore year and even talked about "big league potential." But there was one problem: they wanted me to work hard. They had me running and diving after balls and spending hours in the batting cage.

I played ball at Arizona for the next few years. I played; I didn't work at it. Now, my senior year, I play the bench much more than the field.

People, especially my coaches, are always telling me to get serious. "Sports is like life," they say. "If you don't put 100% into it, you'll get 0% back." You know what? That's crap. My father was an electrician, a union man, who never killed himself on the job. He never made great money, but he did OK. At least he never electrocuted anybody, he'd say. My mom loved him and he was always there for me. In fact, that's how I learned to hit. He was pretty good for an old guy.

I remember when his friend, Jack Constantine, talked him into starting their own business. I never saw him work so hard, even weekends. If he wasn't at a job, he was doing the books or drumming up work. I also never saw him so miserable. He was smart, though. Unlike Jack, he kept up his union dues and when he admitted how miserable he was, he quit the business and the union found him work. "Steady work," I remember him telling me, "it beats worrying about getting rich."

Dad is even thinking of retiring early now that I'm graduating. The scholarship I got helped him out a lot. Just before I got the award, Dad talked to Jack about working for him evenings and Saturdays. He never said anything to me about it, but I knew he was worried about how to pay for college. So when I got the scholarship, Dad was as happy for himself as he was for me. He never liked to work hard. Like father like son, I guess.

I remember when he drove me to the airport after I came home from college my first Christmas break. He said, "Don't worry about being great, son. It's more important to be good. You sleep better." I didn't really understand what he meant at the time, but as I watch my teammates popping pills to get that "competitive edge" and my classmates panicking over their grades, I realize he was pretty smart.

Now, I'm just about ready to graduate, and I sleep just fine. I'll get a degree in English, and I met a girl I'm crazy about. We're planning on getting married when she graduates next year. In the meantime, I'm applying for scholarships to graduate school because I'm in no rush to start a job.

When I get out I'll probably teach—I'd love to work with kids. Maybe I'll do some writing. Just as long as I don't have to break a sweat.

Idle Woe

Hakeem Beedar

In a dark room, Kai sits in silence, shaking his leg. The roof is leaky; each drop of water complements each sharp intake of breath.

"Maybe I should stand." His voice bounces on the walls. Oh, how his joints burn. In contrast, the wall at his back is cold. He cannot feel it. All he feels are the cracks along its brick — the faults that need a push to fall apart.

"Maybe I should go," he ponders aloud. But that would be unjust, wouldn't it?

Footsteps approach and the cell door swings open.

"Kai," says the uniformed man. "It's time."

Gift of Grace

Christine Johnson

Why haven't I found a name that fits? Silly, juvenile maybe, but I've always named my favourite possessions. And this old car is super-special. An unexpected bequest from Grandma Grace, I thought I'd hit the jackpot. I sit in her spot behind the wheel six months on and she still lingers. Her sweet old-fashioned scent brushes the back of my throat. Leather seats crinkle like her cheeks, their folds the raspberry colour of jam she made.

Relax. Foot on the brake, I turn the key. Tut, tut. The engine grumbles, shakes aside sloth, sputters to life. A slow acceleration and I cruise down the drive. My heart beats as I edge out onto the shadowy street. Only once I'm clear of the house do I risk one hand leaving the steering wheel. I reach for the switch. Click. The headlights blaze and I'm off!

Tomorrow morning Mum will sit as usual beside me. She'll offer encouraging words. I'll imagine Grandma's ghost smiling in the back seat as we, all three, set out to sit my final driving test. Coming home triumphant, I'll place my new licence in my purse, next to my boyfriend's photo.

Breathe. I'm not a rule breaker by nature. Only, tonight is my last chance. The act of proving I can do this is important. Just once, I want the thrill of going it alone.

Down the hill and left, left again, head towards the main road. Check the mirrors. Eyes fixed, I focus on the traffic lights ahead. Relieved, I see them flash green as if beckoning me. I sashay through the intersection. Settle back.

Rows of streetlights, sleeping houses, going straight everything feels so, so normal. I'm entering an unblemished beginning. Full of hope I pass the little shop on the corner; follow the road around the oval, think of driving here next Saturday to cheer my boyfriend on. Soccer, that's his thing. I'll have my licence, something special to show my girlfriends.

I wonder what his reaction to my licence will be. We've kissed in my car's backseat while it's been parked in the driveway, going nowhere. He's hinted. Now I sense the air might alter, quickening with sex, urging us, me, to drive elsewhere to sample as-yet secret spaces.

Another junction looms. I slow. Consider. Over the railway, or choose the other way, heading back onto the main road? I've no destination in mind. A brightly lit neon sign grins. I hand-over-hand steer myself that way. Speed bumps. My stomach lurches. Another set. I'm heading around a bend, up a slope.

I brake. There's a line of cars waiting, edging, waiting. No way back. Ahead, a jungle of signs direct to places unknown. Tail lights speed past. Tense, I count. Cars shoot forward. I'm next. Give way. I accelerate forward. A horn slaps the air, screaming. I'm in!

Shaking, I lean forward. Forget driving. Cling to Grandma's name.

'Grace. That's it. I'll call her Grace.'

Three cars enter the tunnel closing too fast. It's instinct. Hit my horn. Find a gap. Swerve.

BANG!

The Speed of Love

Steven Carr

Lloyd entered the front door of his parent's home carrying a red felt banner that had the word "zoo" in large white letters on it. He put it in the umbrella stand that was crammed with a dozen other zoo banners, and sauntered into the living room.

His father was sitting in the Barcalounger with his bare feet up on the footrest and holding a can of beer. He was wearing a t-shirt with a large hole over his left nipple and a pair of white boxers. Both the t-shirt and boxers were stained with mustard, ketchup, pizza sauce and pickle juice. There were empty beer cans, a pizza box, candy bar wrappers, and an empty potato chip bag on the floor around the chair. He was staring at the television, watching football. The volume was up so high that the television's speakers vibrated.

Lloyd sat down on the sofa, kicked off his shoes, and propped his feet up on the coffee table. He took his iPhone from his shirt pocket and stared at the pictures he had taken while at the zoo. His heart raced, his cheeks burned, his eyes glazed over.

Twenty minutes later his father looked over at him and said, "Did you find a job?"

Lloyd pointed to his ear, and then the television, and shouted, "I can't hear you."

"What did you say?" his father shouted back.

This back and forth went on for several minutes before Lloyd's father picked up the remote and turned down the volume.

"Did you find a job?" his father asked.

"It's Saturday. No one interviews anyone for positions on a Saturday. I went to the zoo again."

His father belched. "You've been going to the zoo a lot. Maybe you could find a job there. Certainly someone has to be hired to clean out the cages."

"There aren't any job openings at the zoo," Lloyd said. "I checked."

"You're thirty-one and haven't worked in over a year. All you do is lie around the house, except lately you manage to get dressed and go to the zoo. You should be working."

"You don't work," Lloyd replied.

"I don't have to work. Your mother works. She loves working."

Lloyd looked at the image on his iPhone, sighed heavily, and then stood up. "I'm going to go lie down until Mom gets home," he said.

"You could mow the grass," his father said. "The weeds have overtaken the yard."

"Maybe tomorrow if I don't go to the zoo," Lloyd said as he walked out of the room.

He went into his bedroom. On the way to his bed he cleared a path across the floor as he kicked aside dirty clothes, paperback novels, and empty soda cans. He lay on his unmade bed, held his iPhone up, and stared at the image on the screen. *She's beautiful,* he thought.

He slowly drifted off to sleep.

Lloyd awoke to the sound of his mother's voice.

"Supper is ready," she said.

He opened his eyes and gazed drowsily at her. She was wearing a freshly ironed blouse and a pair of slacks. Her graying hair was pinned neatly on top of her head. "How was your day?" he asked her.

"I spent the day working at the homeless shelter," she said. "How was yours?"

"I went to the zoo."

"Again?"

"I didn't want to say anything before this, but I go to the zoo to meet someone. I think I'm in love. Her name is Grace. She's beautiful." He paused, and then said, "I think she's the one." He picked up his iPhone from his chest. "I plan on asking her to marry me. Would you like to see her picture?"

"Not right now," she said. "The important thing is that you don't make the mistake I made. I love your father, but I didn't realize before I married him how slothful he is. Life with him has been a struggle. Make certain the two of you are compatible in every way."

"We are, Mom," Lloyd said. "Almost in every way, but we're going to take things slow. I don't want to rush into marriage, and I'm certain that's how Grace feels also."

"Your father is already sitting at the table, so wash up and come in and eat," she said, and then turned and left.

Lloyd swung his feet around and sat up on the edge of the bed. He looked at Grace's picture, and kissed the screen. *I've never felt so happy*, he thought.

*

Lloyd went through the turnstile at the entrance to the zoo and fell in behind a throng of senior citizens who had the pathway blocked. Their slow progression as they went by the animal exhibits suited him just fine, despite his pounding heart and sweaty palms. He leisurely looked at zebras, bears, monkeys and antelope while frequently checking his watch. He was to be at the same bench as the times before, at the same time as always, 11:30.

Noticed by an elderly woman with blue tinted white hair, she said to him, "What's a young man your age doing coming alone to the zoo?"

"I'm meeting my fiancée-to-be here," he said.

"Oh, how lovely," she said. "I used to meet my husband at the zoo before we were married. A zoo is a very romantic place."

"Yes it is."

They walked together for a short distance.

At the plexiglass window in front of the sloth enclosure, he said. "I've gotten here just in time."

Upside down, Grace slowly crawled down the small tree inside the enclosure.

"There's my fiancée now, coming down to be fed. Isn't she wonderful?"

"That's a sloth," the woman exclaimed.

"Just like me," he said.

He sat on the bench and gazed lovingly into Grace's sleepy eyes as she pushed yam strips into her mouth with her claws.

Fish 'n' Chips with a Tin of Cheap Beer

Nod Ghosh

I'm tired when I begin my shift. The charge nurse asks me to check on a woman in the far bay. She has bled into her brain.

At first I'm not sure it's her.

I check the notes and wristband and swallow back the tears.

It's her.

Ours was an easy friendship.

We went back to her place that first night. We talked, listened to records and laughed at nothing in particular. The last bus had gone, and I couldn't face walking back to my place, so I crashed on her sofa.

We went to a film the next night, and I stayed at her flat again.

The pattern was set. I started hanging around with her a lot. Late nights watching films, drinking.

I missed essay deadlines, requested extensions for imaginary illnesses, and satisfied myself with mediocre grades. We'd meet for coffee, go to gigs, or talk and listen to records.

We joined the yoga society and would meditate on mats in her bedroom, focussing on imaginary internal suns until the room was suffused with our warmth and colours.

We read books about world religions and spirituality, instead of reading coursework. We spent hours arguing about evolution with the 'God Squad' kids from the Christian Society.

We took the bus to the coast, paddled in freezing water until our feet turned blue. We'd come back with overpriced bottles of peach wine from the sea-front boutiques. Sometimes we would drink the best part of a bottle of spirits between us, and stay up all night solving the nuclear crisis, apartheid or world poverty and be comatose the next day.

She introduced me to sensimilla and I'd make hash cakes in her oven. When we had cash, we'd buy fish 'n' chips, lick the grease off our fingers, and drink tins of cheap beer.

I'd cop off with the odd guy. There was a bloke I'd met at a protest after the Three Mile Island meltdown. We ended up shagging in the women's toilets. It didn't lead to anything. I'd just enjoyed the thrill of the chase. I didn't want a boyfriend. I was having too much fun.

I didn't want a boyfriend unless the guy with the mono-brow was offering.

I liked that guy a lot. We'd danced at a disco once, and I thought he was about to kiss me, when she'd grabbed my arm and taken me to a party. I got so wasted I slept through the whole of the next day.

That guy was everywhere though. He'd come out of the engineering building, folders poking from his backpack.

I saw him in the Union, the laundry, and the pub. We'd smile at each other. Sometimes he'd say hello. I didn't talk to him though. I couldn't. My mouth furred up whenever I was near him.

Once I saw him coming out of her place. Perhaps they'd brushed fingertips when he walked out of the door. Something cracked in my chest. But when I asked who he was, she just said *nobody*.

She never seemed to have a steady boyfriend, though she'd often leave the pub on the arm of some gorgeous individual. I'd bus back to my place on those nights, wondering if the man would usurp my position in her life. But we'd always slip back into our old patterns. I'd go back to her place after the pub, roll a spliff and chat. Sometimes she'd play guitar, and we'd sing. We'd drink, smoke, laugh, and I'd sleep in till noon the next day.

Occasionally I'd turned up at her door and she'd ask me to leave.

"I'm busy," she'd say, holding the front of her dressing gown closed. I'd be cut to the core. But the next time I saw her, we'd take off from where we'd left, as if nothing had happened.

It was like I'd known her my whole life. She understood everything that had ever caused me to doubt myself. She made me feel like I was in charge of my own destiny. We finished each other's sentences. We were so close sometimes it felt like we were the same person. If I was upset, there were tears in her eyes. When she hurt, I bled.

The end of the academic year approached and my grades were in my boots. The possibility of not passing my exams didn't bother me, as long as we could hang around together. It was like being in love, without the complication of sex.

*

Her birthday was approaching, and I told my friend I wanted to get her something special, something that would always remind her of me. She didn't hesitate. She didn't ask to think about it. She didn't insist I save my limited funds. She did none of those things. Straight away, she told me what she wanted, as if she'd been waiting for me to ask.

It wasn't something beautiful young women indulged in back then. What she wanted would guarantee she'd remember me for the rest of her life.

She asked for a tattoo.

I imagined an anchor or stylised heart on her upper arm. But she insisted she wanted something unique. She pulled one of the books of ancient yogic symbols from her shelf.

"I want a design that means something special," she said, "that represents people like us, in this time, here and now, but something that is also infinite and eternal." Together we pored over the images. We chose an ouroboros, to symbolise the Divine Power of Kundalini.

The ouroboros was to wind round her ankle.

After all these years, it still chokes me up thinking of what we had, and what we lost.

At first I wasn't sure it was her. The woman has been in a coma for three days. I check her ankle. There it is, creased and faded, a serpent consuming its own tail; the ouroboros tattoo I gave her for her twenty-first birthday.

The Hammock

Jenean McBrearty

Herman Harker trained a sleepy eye on the source of the commotion interrupting his afternoon nap. She was four, he guessed, a red haired, blue-eyed demon in the throes of ecstasy over a wiggly, furry four-legged being named Sparky. Betty, his wife, called her the spawn of Satan and her family their new next-door neighbors, but Herman called them "stinkbane."

"What do retired people have in common with millennial parents? The next thing you know, they'll be organizing something because that's what neighborhood nuisances do. Block watches, see something, say something groups, or worse yet, they'll request volunteer 'safe' houses for their brats."

Wilson, Herman's good next-door neighbor, identified as such by a six-foot privacy fence, issued the following advice, "Do what I do, don't answer the door."

"Never make eye contact, always be busy, and never answer the door. The three golden rules to being left alone," was Carl's contribution. He lived across the cul-de-sac.

Yet eye contact was exactly what the curly-headed creature expected. "He licked me!" she cried with high-pitched delight.

Herman quickly shut his eye and remained silent. Betty had nagged him to fix the broken slats of their privacy fence, but he never got around to it. This was the second time Sparky had sneaked into his mini orange orchard.

"He tickled me!" she said louder. When Herman opened his eye again, he looked into a face that loomed over him. It belonged to Breanna.

"Are you dead?" she asked.

"I was asleep." But the question, asked by one so young gave him chills. "Do I look dead?"

A tentative hand reached out and gave his cheek a gentle poke. "Yes. You've been here all night. I saw you from my window."

He knew the window she meant. He'd toured the house when it came on the market after ol' man Grant died. It was located in a garret-like room on the second floor that Grant used to store his gun collection and overlooked his backyard. Somebody had replaced Grant's plaid drapes with Disney Dumbo curtains.

"Do your parents know you're outside and unsupervised?" He felt another poke, this time to his tummy.

"When my mama was going to have a baby, her tummy was just like yours."

"I'm not having a baby. My tummy is full of beer." He rolled away from her.

"Oh."

He thought for a moment. He'd seen no evidence of a child younger than Breanna. The other two were seven at least. "What did your mama name the baby?"

She came around him. "Charlotte Rose."

"Where is she now?" His eyes were still closed.

"In heaven. Or in Chicago 'cause she wasn't prayed over right."

He'd heard of people so devout they never said the word hell. "That's too bad."

"She was too bad, Mama said. She cried too much and that's why Mama gave her back to God."

Children think such odd thoughts. "Maybe she was sick."

"No. Mama wasn't sick, she was mad. She's mad all the time. Her kisses are mad."

"Bree? Bree? Come here, now!'

"I have to go."

He rolled over again and watched her scamper off, Sparky glued under her armpit.

"I'm coming," he heard her say.

Had he really been in his hammock all night? Maybe. He'd come home during the Labor Day cul-de-sac party. He remembered feeling tired and maybe he crawled into his canvas cocoon and passed out. But died? He retired at fifty-two, played golf for two more years. Then retired from the world.

"You've gotten fat and lazy, Herman Harker. I've told you a thousand times you're not doing your heart any favors by lying around," his still-employed wife told him more than a thousand times. He rarely made eye contact with her. Rarely answered her. Perhaps Carl was right. There were three rules. He needed to look busy so she wouldn't nag. On the other hand, only Betty's nagging got him to the annual party for free food and beer. That's right. They'd had a fight there. Round 8,650 of a bout spread over twenty-five years.

He stretched. Yes, she left the party too, only in a cab, while he finished his eighth beer. He was sure of it. Only he wasn't. People were dashing about and yelling, but he couldn't understand what they were saying. He needed to lie down.

"Wake up, Herman!"

This time it was Carl, shaking his shoulder. "Wake up, for God's sake!"

"What do you want? First it's the kid and now you. Can't a guy sleep off a hangover in peace?"

"The police are here about Betty. You have to talk to them about the fight she had with your new neighbor. Remember? Betty's in the hospital. The man stabbed her with the barbeque fork. You got in the middle of it, you dumb bastard."

His mind was slowly emerging from his Heineken headache. Had Betty left in a cab or an ambulance? He couldn't remember. All he remembered was he couldn't go because he was so very tired. He'd staggered off to his orchard. "She'll get better and come home or die. There's nothing I can do. Dig up the neighbor's yard. There's a kid buried there. Breanna told me."

"Jesus…man, stop babbling and pull yourself together."

To every entreaty, Herman refused to move and sent every pleader away. And when Breanna, bruised and thin beyond recognition, came to his side and again asked him if he was dead, Herman didn't answer.

"I need your help, Mr. Herman," she whispered as she clutched the crushed Sparky in her hands. "I know your name, now. They said they'd come back for you. Can we go with you?" He didn't answer. She lay beside Herman in the hammock, gently patting his chest over his heart, and as night fell, she fell asleep.

The next morning, a shrill voice screamed the name Breanna from the upstairs window, but she did not answer. No one ever answered. That was the secret of being left alone.

Krum the Artist

Larry Lefkowitz

The questionable character of Maximilian Krim was the result of a minor scandal some years back, in which (I recalled) he had been involved, something about selling copied works of art as originals. ("Jason in pursuit of the golden *fleece*," as Lieberman, my mentor, succinctly put it, for all of his lack of empathy for Greek mythology. He also bestowed on Krim the sobriquet "King *Shmear*" – presumably a play on words on King Lear.) Monet said motifs require seeking, but Krim didn't trouble to look too far. It was said of Krim that he had imitated so many still lives in the seventeenth-century style that the sheen of the pewter plates, the glint on the empty wineglasses and the flash of light on the long neck of the porcelain pitcher were second nature to him.

Sometimes he applied the same technique to nineteenth- and twentieth-century styles to produce Israeli modern still lifes, by adding Israeli motifs, when necessary, to literally complete the picture. As for example in his 'improving' Magritte's *The Great Table* – fortunately for Krim, his clients weren't art connoisseurs. He retitled it *Oranges at the Beach*. The original had portrayed a bowl of apples against a sky blue and clouded and with a scimitar moon, sand and sea in the background. Krim substituted oranges and added a lifeguard stand and two paddle-ball beach players. He eliminated the crescent moon, perhaps he considered it too politically charged.

Bouncing back from the forgeries contretemps (his guiding principle seemingly that of the Russian impresario Sergei Diaghilev: "Success is the only thing that redeems everything and covers up everything"), Krim had become successful as a seller of copied works of art as copies. "My copies are better than the originals," he boasted. "They are charged with a numinous inner life which the originals fail to display." Another attribution to him: "If the forgeries were removed from the museums, their walls would be half empty." It was an indication of our times that forgeries were acquired *because* they were forgeries. Things had almost reached the absurd reflected in Woody Allen's claim that his apartment was hung with Picassos done by Van Gogh. Krim, if not quite capable of approaching the latter feat, might very well pull off a claim that he had a painting of Van Gogh by Picasso. Picasso Krim. Apropos of Picasso (and Krim), Lieberman said with regard to Krim's proclivity for repetition, "Picasso painted 49 bulls, but Krim's not Picasso."

Krim chose to wrap his creative self-deceit in a smokescreen of rants against his critics ("The artist's body radiates light from every wound"), self-aggrandizement and even a self-suggested comparison to Raphael. (Victoria, my sought-after and admirer of Krim, bristled when I pointed out that Raphael allegedly died of amorous excess.) Whereas, in practice, Krim's art fell within the conceptual framework of Thomas Mann's *The Confessions of Felix Krull, Confidence Man.* Krim had gotten so good at playing 'Krim' that it was difficult to say whether he was acting or not. Sometimes with amusing results, as per his shtick (which lasted all of a month) of emulating da Vinci's round-the-clock pattern of three-hour wakefulness followed by 15 minutes sleep, which enabled him to leave art functions in the middle in order to sleep, accompanied by his "a là da Vinci." Under the patina of his elegant imperturbable Olympian displaying of aplomb, there lurked a Yiddish chutzpa.

Krim's personal taste in art, I suspected, ran to paintings such as *The Sultan's Favorite Returning from the Bath*. Schmaltz synergized to sex. He without doubt would claim he was faithful to Picasso's dictum, when asked about the difference between art and eroticism, "But there is no difference." Yet it was another painting – Ashile Gorky's *Diary of a Seducer* – that I invariably associated with Krim, because of its title. I doubted that Krim fancied the abstract expressionist painting, if indeed he was aware of its existence.

I refrained from verbally assailing Krim's taste in Victoria's ear (the felicitous description "*art brut*" hovered on my lips) lest she reply (not for the first time), "You have no taste, Kunzman. Worse, you are a master of bad taste." This was a variation of one of Lieberman's favorite literary critical bashing phrases, "_____ not so much lacks taste as is a master of bad taste." And Krim had good taste? The same Krim who – as Lieberman once enlightened me as a result of Victoria's dragging him from time to time to galleries (including Krim's baroque/art deco decorated "studio") "where she liked to be the center of attention of the *fineshemekers* (hoity-toity) – was fond of delivering the same cigar-waving monologue about 'Rembrandt's subtle blending of light and shadow, of Rubens' sweeping lines and sensuous portrayals of flesh and fabric, of Renoir's soft tones, of Van Gogh's brilliant colors'. All of which techniques," Lieberman added, "Krim had learned to copy onto his canvases, according to need."

As much as I disliked Krim, at times when I contemplated some of his paintings, I felt a degree of awe – a sensation not identical with aesthetic pleasure. Awe at the ambition – at the pulling it off. For all of Krim's foolhardy bravado, there was a touching fearlessness about his artistic life which I would not admit to Victoria, and only rarely to myself (embodied in Krim's pronouncement, "When you come right down to it, all you have is yourself."). This aspect of Krim caused me to think of Picasso's Buste – a portrait of a mustachioed *bravo* sporting a fanciful green hat and caparisoned in a black patterned red cloak and white ruff. Surely Krim (knowledgeable about paintings, whatever his artifice, a knowledge which Lieberman had dismissed, unfairly in my opinion, as "low-style connoisseurship", adding, in a pithy, if uncharacteristic, blend of the French and the Yiddish, "a *petit maven*") was aware of it also. I wondered if Krim identified with the portrait. I would like to have asked him but decided against it. He might take it as a compliment.

Or try to sell me a copy.

Day of the Chlorine Death Cloud

Robert Carlton

Our day generally began around 6:30 am. Jones and I would start off with a pot or two of coffee, usually brewed atop the grounds of previous days unless they were beginning to sprout a bluish fur, at which point we would throw them out and start again. I don't think our boss truly appreciated how much money we saved him on coffee filters. At any rate, by about 7:30, once we were wide awake, we would load the work van and head out, always taking the same route no matter where we were working that day: north on the Loop, out of one industrial area in a small dry town and toward another industrial area in a large wet city. Years of studying the consequences of the Byzantine liquor laws of state, county, and city had resulted in our discovery of and appreciation for the fact that the bars on Harold Haynes Boulevard, just across the river that divided and defined municipalities, opened at 7:00 am. What some might call senseless routine or reprehensible habit we had distilled into profane ritual: before doing any work, we stopped in at the CI Saloon and partook of a single root beer float, consumed with ceremony if not solemnity. Then it was off to the job.

Jones and I had been introduced to this wonderful concoction one day at the Spindletop, which we had found through careful, if largely unconscious analysis of various city limit lines and zoning boundaries. By our reckoning, a bar just had to be there, and so it was. We fell into drinking with another pair of urban adventurers who split up the workday into manageable bits with a few strategically placed alcohol breaks. They gleefully bought the house, which consisted of Jones, the bartender, and me, a round of their favorite miracle of mixology. It was a moment of revelation to Jones and me, dropping a shot glass of root beer schnapps into a mug of beer and throwing the thing back in one sustained gulp. From that day forth our course was set.

The drive from the shop to the bar took us past a huge football stadium, a structure that dominated the flat, featureless landscape around it. The AM-only radio in the van was on, which meant we were listening to news/talk of some sort. The story came on at the same time we noticed the stadium was obscured by a white haze that did not look like fog. It seemed a pool chemical supply warehouse not far from us was on fire. As we got closer to the stadium, the haze thickened.

"Smell that?" Jones asked.

"Like a pool," I said. "Like a cloud of bleach."

"Jesus Christ," Jones said, as the faint whiff of chlorine turned into burning, watering eyes and a distinct irritation in the back of the throat, "it's like a fucking chlorine death cloud."

By the time we got to the bar, we seemed to have passed through the worst of it. Of course, winds could shift, storage tanks could explode, fires could spread. As we sat down to the drinks that awaited us, seemingly before we had even fully entered the room, we had variables to consider. The morning was warm, and the back door of the bar was propped open.

"Smell that?" Jones asked the bartender, Jaymee.

"Yeah," Jaymee said, only mildly interested at this early hour. "What is that?"

"Fucking chlorine death cloud," I said.

Jones and I had rules. We did not work in the rain. We did not work when the temperature dropped below twenty-seven degrees. We did not work in high winds. And we sure as hell did not work when we found ourselves in what was essentially a scenario straight out of an apocalyptic science fiction movie. There were other considerations as well. Jaymee could be a middle-aged, pasty, frumpy woman with wide hips and no breasts one day, and a big-haired redneck beauty queen in western shirt and tight jeans the next. Today she was sporting the latter look. She also had a habit of charging us for a fraction of what we drank. It certainly seemed more fiscally responsible to remain here, enjoying the view, safely out of reach of the chlorine death cloud, paying the same price for six drinks as for one, than to risk our very health by going to work.

At 11:00, MaskAura opens up right next door. Happy hour runs until seven, which means a plastic cup of draw beer, barely cool to the touch and pale as the meth-head waitress who serves it, is only $1.75. It looks like we will all be there, Jones and I, the rest of the dedicated day-drinkers, the sublimely unattractive semi-nudes dancing for dollars, all trying to escape the chlorine death cloud and reveling in the fellowship of impending disaster. Then Jones and I will have to go home at the end of the day and think up some justification yet again why we got nothing done at work today. Somehow I don't think the boss will be too impressed with any of our reasoning to this point.

The Goonies vs The Beatles

Jo Hocking

Oh, Sloth. I loved that malformed mutant with the wiggly ears, single tuft of hair and oral hygiene beyond even Mrs Marsh's chalk snapping talents. Swashbuckling Sloth ripping down the sails of a pirate ship on a knife, hurling his mum overboard, ripping open his shirt to reveal a Superman T-shirt, shoving chocolate bars down his twisted gob … He was at once freaky, weird and really cool.

For a fat, nerdy kid who relished the company of dead pirates and fictitious kids who didn't fit in more with the company of any girls my own age, 'The Goonies' ticked all the boxes. It was even better because we rented it from Video Mania from the glorious weekly rack three years after its original cinema release, so it could be watched over and over again!

Sloth's arguably greatest moment came when he suspended a boulder on his butt to allow the Goonies gang to dash between his tree-trunk thighs to ultimately save the day. But the boulder came down, blocking him from his chubby mate Chunk and trapping him with the bad guys. Sloth's guttural bellow of "Sloth Love Chunk" echoed throughout the cave – and the ages – as an eternal cry of mateship.

Sloth inspired another great act that day. If imitation is the sincerest act of flattery, then juvenile plagiarism must be one of its purest forms. When I was 10, I basically pinched all the cool bits of 'The Goonies' and passed Mr Spielberg's original story off as my own in Creative Writing class. Mr Evans, Year 4 teacher at Woodville Primary, can hardly be blamed. How could he follow the complex plots and narrative nuances of a movie about kids on bikes? The caterwauling Cyndi Lauper soundtrack was probably the aural equivalent of mace for him.

My four-page story has miraculously survived the ravages of moves and marriages in its original booklet format of yellow cardboard, staples and masking tape. The cover is a Faber Castell pencil and texta masterclass in disappointment that makes me wonder whether I should question Mum if she dropped me on my head as a baby. A boy plunges into some icy depths feet-first, about to encounter a treasure chest, some fish and inexplicably, a brown owl. Why no fingers on the hands? Why is the crotch a perfect square? Why do I still draw shoelaces with those bunny ears 30 years later? No one will ever know. The right corner proudly boasts a copyright symbol to prevent anybody else cashing in on this masterpiece. The intellectual property would be all mine if I hadn't taken it from somebody else in the first place.

I called my book 'The Beatles'. I don't think I intended to divert attention from my crimes by ripping off a different group of four lads. To my great shame, I think it was an error – I meant to call it 'The Beetles', an appropriate name for boys scarpering around the subterranean. Delving through the text is a history lesson in late 80s computing – behold the dot matrix printing and sausage-fingered typos from the 1988 Amstrad with a fresh 'computer license'.

So, did Sloth perpetuate sloth in a 10-year-old lazily regurgitating the film? Perhaps it was less sloth and more homage to the film in the fashion of a remake. (That's the story if Warner Brothers isn't convinced by the copyright symbol.) None of the girls made the cut and I kept only four boys with different names. The kids in the film are on the hunt for treasure, find a skeleton identified as Chester Copperpot, pull a string that triggers a booby trap of cascading boulders, solve a piano puzzle constructed of bones, jettison preciously down a waterslide with tree roots sticking out everywhere. The kids in The Beatles do all those things (in my defence, the waterslide was particularly cool).

However, there are distinct points of difference between the Astoria original and the cheap Aussie knock-off. For starters, I improved it by adding piranhas! Sadly, I wasted this plot device by allowing the terrible shoelaces to survive. No word on the brown owl. The dead pirate in the film was One Eyed Willy – I called the pirate ship in my story the Five Eyed Frank. Nice work. Spielberg will never know.

As for Sloth? He's not credited with an appearance in the local remake. But his enduring lesson in mateship perhaps inspired an act of legitimate creativity from the young pen (or Amstrad) of Hocking. Instead of a happy Hollywood ending, the boys trigger a booby trap and "are now floating skeletons" in the ship's dungeons. Mates united in their stupidity forever. Sounds like most of the prepubescent boys on bikes I knew.

Communication

Paul Beckman

My future wife likes to leave me notes instead of having discussions, which she insists are detrimental to relationships. She went away for a long weekend with her best friend for a *Mind Sourcing Retreat*—whatever the hell that is.

Friday note
Honey, while I'm away for this three-day weekend please pick up all of your clothes and wash them. You've been wearing the same tighty whiteys for over a week now. Also, please wash everything and I will fold and put your clothes in their dresser and closet upon my return. I'd suggest taking your shirts to the dry cleaners and you can always take your wash to Bubbles, the Wash and Dry place and leave it there and they will wash and fold everything that's not supposed to be dry cleaned. Also, even though it's less expensive to use Martinizing don't do it. Martin will have to get by without you supporting him.

Friday note #2
Hi Honey– I know you love both your Harley and your 56" TV but it's time to choose which one you are going to use. Please pick up all of the Harley parts and tools and try to put them neatly in the garage. If you go to watch TV and can't find the remote I suggest you try your Harley parts since they're supposed to be in the same place. Also, when the hog is out of

the house call Stanley Steemer and they will come over and shampoo the grease out of the rug. I spoke to them and they can do it.

Friday note #3
Hi– I went to get a cup of tea and you're not only out of tea, sugar, and honey, but also out of teacups and all your other dishes. Every dish in the house is either in the sink, dirty as hell, or in the overflow pile on the floor which I've seen you go to when I bring Chinese food over. Yes, that's why I eat from the carton. Call my cleaning lady, Anna at 353-4352 and she will show up with her top crew and get your kitchen spanky clean.
Friday—No more notes

Saturday note #1 1pm
Hey– I bet you just got out of bed and are hungover. I'm going to assume you didn't get to all of yesterday's chores and went out drinking instead. Finish Friday's lists and text me that you have done them and called all on the list. Sheets. Your sheets have turned brown from constant usage. Take all your sheets and pillowcases to the laundry and have them wash and fold. Leave your bedroom window open to get rid of the smoke smell. Take all of the shit off the steps: books, toiletries, shit in paper bags I don't know about or care to hear.

Saturday—Note # 2
Listen Harry. This stuff is not going to get done by itself and neither are you. Have you noticed our lack of sex these past couple of months? Strange how they coincide with you not taking showers, brushing your teeth, or washing your hands plus other things in the hygiene department. Get with it. I expect to see a clean sparkly Harry Monday night.

Sunday Note #1

Dipshit– this stuff is not going to get done by itself and I am not going to help any more than my notes have. I know your lovable NY Giants are playing the hated Patriots today but if you work hard to finish all the chores in these notes you'll have time for your fantasy football.

Sunday Note #2

Put all the garbage out for pickup tomorrow and cash all the empty beer bottles in and you'll be a rich man and have enough money to buy yourself a running back that doesn't say oops quite as often.

Sunday Note #3

Go back to Note #1 and make sure everything on the list is done or almost done. If you didn't have my cleaning lady do the refrigerator throw everything out and clean it and go shopping to fill it and check the expiration dates.

Monday Last note– Speaking of expiration dates yours is up today at 6 pm when I get back.

Monday – The real last note. I drove up to the house and saw my cleaning lady sitting in her car crying and her three helpers shaking their heads no. I saw the Stanley Steemer truck and another truck with a large dead roach on its back atop the truck. The dry cleaner was picking up bags of clothes as was the Laundromat. I'll just bet these excuses are doozies. You must feel proud to have a couple of hundred beer bottles on your porch.

So, Pigpen, this is my goodbye gift to you—not that I'm paying for it but my trip was to find a new place to live in a new city where I have a new job. I'm starting off clean and that takes you out of my life. I can't say I'm going to miss you because I'm not. I can't wait to get to my new apartment with its huge Jacuzzi and soak you out of every pore in my body.

Very Truly Yours,

Me

This Will Come in
Handy One Day

Alex Reece Abbott

Teetering videotape towers scrape the ceiling – formats long obsolete. Not that he can see a video-player. Ziggurat stacks of cassettes, cases cracked, plastic windows dust grimed. Middens of rusting tomato tins – rinsed, stripped of lids and labels, and jammed with pens, long extinct. Ranges of crap mountains that he dreads traversing.

Crossing the threshold of the old man's apartment, Matt fears the mess will consume him, the way amyloid plaques have devoured his father's neurons and *his* mother's before him.

Foisty air swamps him. He'll turn down the heating...if he can find the thermostat.

He shoves aside the blaring headline.

MAN CRUSHED BY PILE OF CRAP.

Ten years ago, he'd been so pleased to find him a place here. Not too institutional. Low maintenance, the right size. Winner of a prestigious design prize for sheltered housing. Now the place is rammed with clutter, an archipelago of junk, each atoll linked by a causeway of crap. He grimaces. What would his house-proud grandmother have said if she'd seen the state of it?

He nudges his way to the bay and heaves open a window but it's inescapable, the growing sense that he's connected to this sloth, this chaos.

He could be crushed by crap at any time.

DAD: MY PART IN HIS DOWNFALL.

Drawing the cool, fresh air into his lungs, Matt makes himself face the task ahead.

Trays running over with past payslips, bank statements, letters. Coins and calendars that are obsolete. Rinsed sardine cans wait, metal tongues furled.

Nothing of value.

He winces at his old man's lifetime of thrift. All those jokes about his miserliness, long pockets, crowbars needed to pry open his wallet. How he'd joined the others, calling him Scrooge.

MAN KEEPS EVERYTHING FROM NEARLY EIGHT DECADES.

His eyes skitter, searching the piles for cause and effect. This is on you. You should have tried to find out, started the conversation.

No crowbar big enough for *that* job, whines his inner judge. You know he didn't do childhood or feelings, Matt.

You are complicit, snaps the judge. You deserve this, Matthew.

Matt scans the room. Nothing of sentiment. Nothing personal.

He crunches a mint.

It tastes stale.

SON REAPS REWARD FOR NEGLECT.

Matt looks out the window. The *cul de sac* is so manicured it could be Stepford.

Each time he makes the trip here, the clammy, dark fug draws in. By the time he reaches the edge of town – marked by the roundabout commandeered by a flock of unintentionally kitsch seabird sculptures – he's fighting the urge to do a total three sixty. Foot flat to the floor for home. Leave the swarming tourists sucking up the flinty, medieval ruins and half-timbered houses, the charming guildhall and haunted pubs.

In this pilgrimage town on the commuter belt, the res is now so des that most locals are priced out. The smug, solid houses with their extensive gardens have names that smack of borrowed dynastic grandeur. *Clarendon. Cliveden. Balmoral.*

Or they invoke roses-around-the door bliss. *Delamere. Bella Vista.*

Matt breaks out another mint.

Sans Souci, my arse.

SON RENAMES DESIGNER SHELTERED APARTMENT *THE DUMP.*

During the move to this place, he'd thought he'd negotiate some downsizing with the old man.

Each item was fraught with debate. He'd tried distracting him, while slipping duplicates – surely indisputable – and junk into the boot of the car, ready for a covert tip trip.

His father matched his subterfuge with stealth, targeting the piles for the bin and reclaiming each item. Wheeling around, hands full, snarling.

What have you got there?

I paid good money for that.

What are you doing with that?

That will come in handy one day – his ultimate rebuttal.

Who could argue against that possibility?

One day.

He'd always liked getting his own way.

Flaming well put that back where you got it. Leave it.

All of it, returned to Crap Mountain. Exhausted, Matt had caved.

Caved. Cave.

Lair.

An expert on the radio said it was a serious illness. Isolating and life-threatening. The risk of being trapped under a toppling pile. Or fires.

Paralysed by indecision, an incapacity greater than his stroke. Distress at letting objects go. A tendency to overthink. Using objects for emotional insulation, or to fill a void.

What was the trigger for such chaos?

Matt evades the accumulations of crap, the same way he's sidestepped the issue. Sidestepped *him*.

The prospect of turning domestic archaeologist churns his gut. Classification as a disorder has an advantage; it has spawned a profession. He'll wade through the jumble in the ether and find a local specialist de-clutterer. She'll sort it all out.

FINAL BETRAYAL
CRAP ONLY CHILD SUB-CONTRACTS HOUSE CLEARANCE.

In the chaos, Matt sees no neat narrative, gains no insight into the forces that have shaped his father.

He arranges this situation into tidy groups, sets them within a soothing Venn diagram...his mind swirls into a five-setter with congruent ellipses. *Son. Parent. Engineer. Father. Descendant. Migrant. Carer. Guardian. Procrastinator. Pedant. Neat-freak. Failure.*

He shudders at the possibility of some logical relationship...him – the old man – the state of this apartment. The union is empty. They do not intersect. Nothing in common, definitely no overlap.

Abandoning schematics and set theory, he reaches for his car keys. Cold and hard and true they are where they should be, in the hip pocket of his jeans.

SON DENIES LINK TO CRAP-HEAP.

Refusing to be overwhelmed, Matt edges towards the front door, snagging his ankle on a protruding egg carton. An avalanche topples, and a battered wooden box spills its guts on the mottled carpet.

When did the old man ever smoke cigars – and why the hell has he held onto an old cigar box?

Cautiously, he bends and scoops the spilled innards. Newspaper clippings, fading till receipts, paperclips and snaking shoelaces.

His fingertips brush a plain circle, worn thin.

He knows the smooth gold at a glance. His grand-mother's...*his* mother's...wedding ring.

He stands beside the open window and phones his boss.

Sorting through this will take longer than he thought.

Lawd the pressure

Mbeke Waseme

She sat drinking the soup. It was warm and kind. She needed a warm and kind experience. She had sent back the burger. They described it as grilled on the menu and yet it was seeping with oil. She explained to the young waiter who seemed shocked and traumatized that she should complain of the food standard in a health food store. He went to seek support in the hope that she might change her mind. It wasn't about to happen for she needed somewhere to place her anger and her shock. She needed an outlet and there was no one at home to go to and to explain what the doctor had said.

The phone was handed to her. The manager apologized and listened attentively. Joanne lost count of the times that she said she was sorry. Joanne was quite clear. The doctor had called her out for not looking after herself and she was stopping it right now. She wanted a grilled healthy burger because she didn't want to die. Other waitresses came and stood around as she spoke to the manager. Her English accent made them stop for they had not met people with brown skin and English accents. They stopped, for this woman was not apologizing for taking breath and space on the planet. An experience they had exploited in the company of other brown people.

No, I don't want to speak to your PR department. Were they looking for free training she wondered? If so, they were cold calling at the wrong door. *It is quite simple. You are deceiving the customers and in this social media world, I could easily tweet and inst your company for a few moments where you'll lose credibility!* Yes yes, I know you could and I hope you'll forgive us and not go down that road.

One of the young waitresses was smiling too much as Joanne spoke. Maybe this Lilly person had been mean to her at some point in their careers together. Karma is such a bitch so you never know where the lesson will come from.

Just change the friggin wording!

She sipped on the soup thinking about the man (who probably wanted to sleep with her) saying he had read her palm and that she was denying herself too many pleasures. He was partially right. She knew that having a son and daughter out there in the world, fending for themselves, made her proud and petrified her too. The world seemed so hard and they seemed so small in the vastness of it all. How many times had she looked closely at the 'young man caught on camera'. She had to look closely as they all wore the same hairstyle, jeans, and black jackets.

You haven't been looking after yourself.

So what the heck was the walking, yoga, healthy eating, staying away from the Tel lie vision?? Secretly she knew though. She disliked her job and her boss was a passive-aggressive tyrant. He had an army of scared protegées who jumped to his every request. It was that rather than feel the brunt of his army's exclusion and silent oppression. Joanna had not cared. In her life, she wore her usual bright and bold African clothes, danced her African dance and lived her African dreams. This man could not be at peace with her and made her life hell. On many days, she experienced a small axe chipping away at her confidence and self-esteem. In that boxing rink, Joanne got up and came back, every time he thought he had knocked her out.

You could damage your heart, your kidney, and your brain. A stroke could happen. The levels are dangerously high.

She wanted to run away and to not listen anymore. It was enough for one evening. In fact, it was too much. She wanted the tablets now. She would take them, all of them and then detox when her body was again acting the way she was used to. He spoke about her taking the tablets for life which was not her plan. She accepted the seriousness of this here and now result though. Taking tablets for life was not in the script. She was entitled to good health. She would have good health.

She enjoyed the soup and drank it slowly. A plate of grease, even if the ingredients had been plant-based, was not going into her temple today. She had work to do, people to inspire, books to write and speeches to be shared.

The chef came out and explained that the *buns* were grilled. Joanne didn't respond for the damage had already been done. Four, five, probably six of the staff passed her table as she ate to ask *Is everything alright, madam?* She nodded as she enjoyed her simple soup and tomato baguette. Yes, the soup may have been contaminated because she had complained but it was a chance she was willing to take.

Her blood had felt pressured in exactly the same way it would have been had she been eating fried food, doing no exercise, smoking, drinking alcohol and taking lots of salt in her food. He told her not to exercise, not for a few days at least and to come back! He prescribed the same tablets that he was taking. He, the doctor.

The doctor at the acupuncture center had said she'd have to see her allopathic doctor for the gentle Chinese medicine had not worked. The western conditions had produced this, so western medicine would cure it.

Waiting for the bus, she decided that this evening would be one of no worry. No hurry and no bad curry. She would simply be a sloth.

Game On

Sharron Hough

Maryanne re-wrapped her cardigan around her and retied it with its woollen belt. Her nose subconsciously wrinkled at the damp stale air in the room. Antiquated telemetry machinery beeped in syncopated rhythm with beads of water dripping from the ceiling.

Another room they would have to vacate soon, she thought.

The fix was probably a simple one, blocked gutter or cracked tile, but getting anyone out to do the work would mean being placed on a waiting list for over six months and it costing more than a month's worth of wages. It was easier to vacate the room.

She pulled the chart from the end of the bed and went through the checklist. Though his pulse was still strong and his breathing regular, it was clear the patient's muscles were showing signs of atrophy. She checked the calendar. *Four more days.*

Maryanne paced the room. There was nothing more she could tidy, nothing else she could check. She contemplated climbing up and fixing the roof herself, but her insurance, if there were such a thing, probably wouldn't have covered her injuries if she fell. Nobody was covered any more. Nobody covered the risk, so nobody took the risk. Unless you were willing to pay extra.

The few tradies who continued to work, inflated their prices to cover their own safety and health. Others, unwilling or unable to re-train, gave up and joined the queues of unemployed and depressed.

Big pharma struck it rich riding on the downtrodden souls of the dispirited and despondent as the demand for mental health medication skyrocketed. Trial studies boomed as thousands who needed money were willing to become guinea pigs for the right price.

Jeremy was one of the ones willing to take the risk. As part of the trial study, Maryanne was assigned to monitor him in his own home.

The drug was the brainchild of the pharma company Slayer. Slothotol was a twilight drug designed for the long-term use of the clinically depressed. Placing the patient in a dream-like state, Slothotol was used to open all brain channels for re-programming. A urinary catheter was inserted along with a feeding tube and oxygen mask. The patient was monitored hourly, their vital signs checked and recorded and if ever they showed signs of distress, the counter drug Hyperfol could be administered via IV to wake the patient into consciousness again.

A virtual reality mask was worn along with noise cancelling headphones. While they were in the dreamlike state, a series of subliminal re-programming recordings was played. Electrodes placed to read brain impulses, controlled choices within the programs. For the trial, the drug was only used in conjunction with self-help programs, but the view was to introduce retraining modules for those who found traditional methods of learning difficult.

Jeremy had been on the drug for three weeks. The longest a patient had been on the trial was for eight weeks, resulting in several weeks of rehabilitation for the patient on the other side to build up muscle strength.

Running her eye over her meticulous notes, Maryanne had noticed irregular peaks and troughs in Jeremy's blood pressure and pulse rate. Though a slight elevation in blood pressure was an expected contraindication of the drug, the racing pulse wasn't, but as it always returned to normal fairly quickly, she didn't feel the need to pull him from the trial.

A flurry of sudden arm movements sent the chart in Maryanne's hand flying. Jeremy had been prone to excessive twitching and muscle movement throughout the trial. Again, not a known side effect of the drug, but as he seemed well in other areas, Maryanne recorded her findings, suspecting it was a patient-specific reaction.

Picking up the DVD cover of the self-help disk, Maryanne pondered at what information was recorded to provoke such intense movement in Jeremy's limbs. *It wasn't a dance DVD* she thought, *maybe it was 'Believe in Yourself Boxing'.*

Telemetry sirens screamed as a spike in Jeremy's blood pressure registered. Still skittish from Jeremy's mid-air arm assault, Maryanne jumped, sending the disk cover clattering against the wooden floor. Opening on impact, the self-help disk dislodged itself and wheeled its way across the floorboards wavering slightly before landing.

What the?

Puzzled as to what could be in the player, Maryanne searched the room. She couldn't pull the disk from the player: that would have sent Jeremy into shock. She checked inside the bedside drawers, and under the bed before she spotted it, wedged firmly between the bed and the drawers: Sky Sim, The Zelda Scrolls.

Three weeks of completely uninterrupted gaming. No bathroom breaks, no meal breaks and a nurse to watch over you. The ultimate gaming experience.

Slayer had just hit the jackpot.

The Wise Call it Sloth

Robin Hillard

Elder was pleased, the project was going to plan. In a few more cycles the atmosphere Up Top would support their life.

He passed the record to his assistant, who barely glanced at the graph. "I don't know why we bother," he said. Like most of the community Young had little interest in Up Top where huge organisms were reputed to thrive in the poisonous, oxygen rich conditions.

Instead of lecturing Young, Elder brought out the munchies, and leaned back, to signal a break. While they enjoyed the small treat, he talked about The Bigs. Those weird, aerobic creatures of unbelievable size, like the agglomerations of rock. It was hard to credit such bulk could sustain life, and even harder to believe that the mass could have coherent thought. But it was true.

"Most of the planet is aerobic," Elder said, "Aren't you worried that our life is confined to such a small part of The Deep?"

Young's body shook a negative. For one who'd never known the vastness of Up Top, the habitat seemed world enough. Why bother to colonise the aerobic space?

That view was not unpopular. It had been hard to make the Council move. Like every organism, its members carried a resistance to change. This gives stability, but in excess, leads to inertia, a laziness the Wise call sloth. The Council would have been happy to drift in comfortable inaction if the Wise had not prevailed. But they did prevail and the Council built him a large, wonderfully crafted vessel, filled with their own good atmosphere, and capable of buzzing through the poisonous air Up Top.

"I can't believe you weren't squashed by the Bigs!"

Elder rippled with laughter. "The Bigs are too large to notice my ship," he said. "They took it for one of their own small forms of life and it buzzed around, like one of their flies. As long as they think intelligence requires a large mass, our size makes us invisible."

The aerobic world was spectacular, with oxygen creating flora, huge fauna—and the Bigs. In many ways the Bigs were like himself, and were it possible to use the same physical space, intellectually they could meet as friends. Not something Elder would say to Young. Nor would he tell his assistant how he mourned the large, colourful forms that would be lost in the changing atmosphere. "It is them or us," he said.

Because the Bigs were building vessels to befit their size, filled with their own, poisonous atmosphere. How long before they plumbed the anaerobic Deep?

"And there is a greater threat." He took another munchie and passed one to Young before continuing. "As yet, even if the Bigs find anaerobic life, they won't expect intelligence in anything smaller than their own wet mass. But they're already using nano-particles, and, in time they'll recognise the possibilities of different life.

"And, after that, how long will it be before they realise their own, electrically powered brainwaves can be hacked?" For it was the thoughts he planted in those brains, working on the greed of the Bigs that was moving the atmosphere towards a liveable state.

"Hacking?" Young snorted. "The council must be insane. How many minds do they think you can reach, buzzing around in your vessel? If Up Top is as huge as you say, and the Bigs as numerous, it's a hopeless task. You think infecting a few with greedy ideas will change a world. How long before they notice the depleted atmosphere and effect a reversal?"

"The few have infected others with their greed. And as for the numerous hordes you talk about—we needn't be too worried about them. Reversal takes sacrifice and effort."

"They'll make the sacrifice," Young quoted Elder's stories back to him. "Once they see the destruction and their scholars sound the alarm, they will mobilise. Look at their wars."

"Sacrifice, yes—they'll give their young to a fight, but a reversal needs more than a sudden sacrifice. It requires deprivation and hard work. Let the scholars scream. It'll take more than that to make the masses move. And even when they know the remedy, the Bigs won't move to save their atmosphere."

Elder gave silent thanks for the lassitude, so ingrained in the Bigs, that The Wise called Sloth.

The Recent History of the Sánchez Family Tragedies: Part IV

Guilie Castillo Oriard

Seems I owe you an apology. I never imagined you'd take the whole thing so personally, given your own history with the family. You contacted me, you said you wanted to know, and no one else would (or could) tell you. It was never my intention to cause you any distress. You must believe that, even if you believe nothing else.

About that. Look, I understand your decision to end all correspondence with me, and I'll abide by it. But after the accusations you made you can't have imagined I'd fade obediently into silence.

I'm not so much offended as intrigued. The last time I saw you, you were maybe five, and I must've been twenty-five. That's half my lifetime ago. Neither of us much resembles who we were then. Neither of us knows much about the other's life, the things that made us into who we are now. I do wonder: what made you so distrustful? And what life do you imagine I've lived that I'd take pleasure from inventing such sordidness about the blood we share?

I *am* a storyteller. Your father can tell you: I always wanted to be a writer. My imagination was the driving force behind all those fantastic games of pretend that shaped so much of our childhood. Yes, in retelling the family history I've had to fill in gaps: none of us were there. And I can see how you might imagine the resulting story is my wannabe novelist at work.

It isn't. My reconstruction may be embellished, but it isn't pure conjecture.

After your great-uncle Toño was murdered and Anselmo, your grandfather, disappeared, your father inveigled me into going through Anselmo's house and placing anything 'important' into safekeeping. (Your father was living down in Oaxaca; this was a couple of years after your mother left him for—well, I'm not sure how much you know about that.) I didn't want to do it; the last time my mother and I visited Anselmo, some five years before the murder, we had to climb, literally, over piles of mildewed boxes to get past the door—and the rest of the house didn't look any better.

Your grandfather was—well, some would call him a hoarder. When Anselmo put something away, Maura used to joke, the 'where' was his and God's, but when it came to finding it again, the 'where' was only God's. Her other children smiled and nodded and, when she wasn't looking, rolled their eyes. Toño's fussy perfectionism was legendary. His sisters all ran pristine households that ran like clockwork. Maura herself got antsy at even a hint of clutter. In fact, both the Sánchez and the Haley sides of the family seem to have fastidiousness as a common trait.

Except Anselmo. Just another thing to set him apart.

My mother, Anselmo's youngest sister, blamed Maura. She had spoiled him, she said, and maybe that's all it was. Or maybe it went deeper. I remember him vibrant, laughing, blue eyes sparkling as he played Maura's favorite Scottish ballads on the guitar. But underneath that vitality there was a passivity, a kind of indolence. Always full of energy until actual effort had to be expended. Until the novelty wore off. Great at making promises, awful about keeping them. He struggled to finish projects, plans, even books.

All that clutter in his house wasn't 'hoarding'; I don't think he had any active intent of holding on to anything at all. It was as if he'd figured that keeping everything was the path of least resistance. No sorting, no decision-making on what to throw out.

It took me two weeks to find what your father—bless his pragmatic soul—would have considered 'important': the property deeds (in a moth-eaten cardboard box, mixed in with kindergarten drawings, grade school report cards, a heavily highlighted copy of *A Tale of Two Cities*, that kind of thing) and utility bills (some rolled up in a coffee tin labeled to expire in 1972, and others in a series of plastic shopping bags, along with a collection of receipts—a memorable one at the top was for a crate of Coca-Cola bought at *El Sardinero*, a supermarket chain that disappeared sometime in the '80s, I think).

I found the plastic bags in the 'workshop'. You remember that bare-concrete half-finished bunker at the back, behind the two pine trees? Your father and I used to climb those pines; 'the castle', we called them. And in the background of all my memories of our 'pretend'—I the princess, he the pirate (we made it work, somehow)—always the sound of sawing and hammering from that outbuilding: your grandfather building something, fixing something. Another project doomed to incompletion.

The door opened only a crack; three makeshift shelves had collapsed against it. Generations of rats and raccoons and birds had lived—and died, judging by the smell—there. The stench of feral urine and rodent cadavers, of kerosene and solvents and rotting wood, stuck to the back of my throat for weeks.

The plastic bags had been crammed into the back of a cabinet. I found the box behind the bags. At first I thought it was only instruction manuals and warranties for Anselmo's tools, once top of the line, now probably unserviceable. If the sunlight from the grimy window behind me hadn't caught the edge of a lighter, older, thicker paper under the Makita booklets at the top, the Sánchez family history might have faded into the blandness of ordinary lives.

Photographs, even some sepia ones, with abbreviated notations in the back. Birthday cards spanning a century. Old envelopes with British postage, stamped AIRMAIL. Postcards from three continents. Letters, some brief (from Maura's sisters, who wrote in polite, unoriginal language), but many lengthy: Papa Haley's sister, Maureen, wrote to her brother of the farm in Scotland (and asked after 'the boy'—had to be Anselmo, I think). Papa Haley wrote to Maura—probably during the years she and The Doctor spent in Durango—and even some of Maura's replies.

It's all there. Some of it is spelled out, much is implied—references to conversations, allusions to what someone knew or didn't know, promises, advice. Like pieces of a jigsaw, jumbled and, sure, maybe incomplete: possibly an eye is missing, an earring or a table corner, forever blank. But the rest of the picture—well, that would still be identifiable, wouldn't it?

Mae

Tom Fegan

I sat across from Mae Brinks-Fisk, Human Resources Manager at Aerodynamics.

Aerodynamics, a defense industry contractor nestled in a suburb of Dallas, Texas, neighbored the Dallas Naval Air Station and was the U.S. Navy's primary contractor for fighter jets.

This corporation was Mae's jungle kingdom. The petite brunette had caressed her way into this position, just as she had done with everything. Mae Brinks-Fisk knew the angles and how to play them. This had become apparent to all our college classmates when we were studying Business Administration together.

"I always admired your eagerness," she began tensely. "As well as your concern for getting things done like those school projects we did together. You have a talent for business management. It was you who helped get us through those days." She paused. "However, such talent can be a liability as well as an asset."

"Why?" I asked smugly.

"Do you know what this plan of yours would do to this place?" she asserted.

"How this business should be operated?" I asked, my sarcastic tone adding salt to the moment.

The former campus icon leaned forward and glared. She had charmed her way to student council positions, scholarships, and was always seen with the right man. Mae married one, too. Hamilton Fisk, a middle aged confirmed bachelor ... until he met her. He was also Vice President of Plant Logistics and my department head.

My post-college career started at Winston Steel. It was the beginning of my introduction into Physical Distribution, also known as Traffic Management. I was promoted to Traffic Supervisor but an economic downturn saw me join the ranks of the unemployed. Ronald Reagan was President and the Marines were in Beirut as part of a multinational peacekeeping force. The mission was to promote a ceasefire between the warring Muslims and Christians. I needed a paycheck and Aerodynamics hired me.

The distinct difference between the two industries shocked me. Employees were never stressed or tired but resented any extra effort required of them. Management created a façade of job activity. Data entry at computers as well as many other duties were allocated so that three people did one person's job. It was true at my desk. I marveled that jet fighters were ever built and flew efficiently.

Contracts were awarded to sub-contractors and suppliers that bid low but nevertheless charged extravagantly for their offerings; generally, a payoff was suspected but not investigated. Government "watchdogs" hired to regulate and protect taxpayer dollars funding the company were ignorant as to what to investigate. It was a taxpayer rip-off. This fact became obvious to me as I shuffled paper and studied the information and files at my desk.

At his monthly departmental meeting Hamilton Fisk summed up: "Aerodynamics is strong and moving forward." He paused and related the news of a Marine Corps Lieutenant who drew down on three Israelis Tanks with his .45. Tension was mounting in Beirut. "This is good news for us! What we need now is a good war!" Fisk concluded.

Laughter and applause followed.

I was sickened by the response and by Fisk as well. At lunch in the cafeteria a sign drew me away from my Chef Salad. It invited employees to submit ideas that would aid in improvements for the company. This included safety or efficiency. All suggestions were to be sent to Human Resources. A bounty of one hundred dollars was offered for the best suggestion. It took me a week but I followed through and ended up in front of Mae Brinks-Fisk with her scowling expression.

"You don't realize the upset you have created," Mae remarked.

My plan was to cut the fat in personnel, suggesting that the government reps should be experienced businessmen and auditors. This would keep expenses down, enabling the jet fighter to be properly priced, and therefore create taxpayer savings.

"You need to get on board and do your job," she added. "The only reason you're still working here is because we went to business school together. But you've crossed a line this time."

I nodded and smiled, knowing I would not be awarded the one hundred dollars.

Mae would stay with this company, I knew. It was her gold mine. After many years of employment with Aerodynamics, she would earn a retirement pension and kick back.

But I resented receiving a paycheck while basically idle, and while young men and women were in harm's way overseas.

As for me, it was official: Hamilton Fisk did not want me around.

The meeting was over.

The following day I resigned and joined the Marines.

The Return of Red Ledbetter

Episode 4: Tattoo Man

JP Lundstrom

When Detective Red Ledbetter arrived on the scene, his partner, Leo Wilson, was already kicking in the door of apartment 808.

"Police!" Ledbetter entered, his gun at the ready.

Standing over a man's body, a pistol in her trembling hands, was Belle Charmant.

"I didn't do it!"

Ledbetter glanced at the body that lay amid a clutter of takeout containers, pizza boxes and assorted cans and bottles. The man fit Miss Kitty's description: about five ten, he looked to weigh around 240 pounds. Black hair fell over closed eyes, but didn't hide the star-shaped scar on his left eyebrow. Both arms were heavily covered with the artistry of Samoan tribal tattoos. He wore a green shirt, emblazoned on the back with a golden dragon and the words 'Chinese Food' in Mandarin.

He had found the tattooed Chinese delivery man.

Ledbetter's gaunt face showed no emotion. "Put the gun down, Miss Charmant."

Wilson peered at him. "You know her?"

Ledbetter turned to answer. "We've met."

They heard the girl's weapon hit the floor, followed by the thump of a body. She was out cold, lying on a pile of old magazines.

Wilson started forward. "You scared her."

"Stop!"

Wilson froze. "What?"

"Check the victim first. Don't step on anything." While Wilson knelt beside the body, Ledbetter approached the only other door. Cautiously, he pushed it open. A bedside lamp showed the room to be empty, except for more cans and bottles. He checked the closet and bathroom, finding only mildew.

Someone groaned.

"Ouch! That hurts." The man on the floor opened his eyes. His hand went to his head and came away bloody.

"Tagata Pe'a?"

"Yeah. Call me Tag. What happened?"

"That's what we'd like to know." Wilson answered as he helped the man sit up. "We kicked in your door—"

"You *what?* Oh, man! They're gonna make me pay for that."

"Couldn't be helped," said Ledbetter. "We heard gunshots."

"Gunshots?" Tag spotted the woman on the floor. "Somebody shot Belle?"

"No, Brainiac," Wilson pinched the bridge of his nose. "Somebody shot you. That's how you wound up on the floor."

"Then what's the matter with her?"

"She fainted when my partner pulled a gun on her."

The man scowled at Ledbetter. "What's the matter with you? You don't pull a gun on a defenseless woman!"

"Easy, fella. We're the good guys. I'm Detective Wilson, and that's Detective Ledbetter."

"Still. Why'd he pull a gun on her?"

Red answered. "We heard shots, came in, and found her with a gun in her hand. Standard procedure."

"You guys are too much. Help me up."

"Stay down." Wilson looked out on the alley before closing the curtains. "Let the shooter think he succeeded."

"The shooter's not out there. We heard it. It came from in here." Ledbetter eyed the woman. "She could be acting…"

Belle moaned. Her eyes opened. "What happened?"

The delivery man answered. "You fainted, Belle."

Her eyes grew rounder and she sat up. "Tag! You're all right!"

"Just a scratch," he chuckled, touching his wound gingerly. "I have a hard head."

"Thank God!" She scrambled across the littered floor and hugged him. "I thought you were dead."

"You want to tell us what's going on here?" Ledbetter's voice was cold.

Belle turned ocean-blue eyes on him. "I came to show Tag my Christmas gift from Grandmère."

"She calls me Tag." He smiled.

Belle pushed papers aside on the floor. "Where did it go?"

Wilson held up the gun. "This it?"

"Yeah, that's it," Tag said.

"It's empty." Wilson dropped the gun into an evidence bag.

"But Grandmère says I need it for protection."

Ledbetter wound a 'hurry-up' sign in the air. "Then what happened?"

"Well, then somebody shot Tag, you came in, and I fainted."

"What's this all about?" Tag wiped soy sauce from a spilled packet off his hand and onto his shirt.

Wilson helped first Tag, then Belle stand. Some dusty thing caught in her hair.

"We were called about a dead man in the alley. When I was directed to apartment 808, the woman there was shot and killed—"

"Luz is dead?" Tag rubbed his forehead, then hissed in pain.

"Then somebody shot you. Is there someone who would want to injure both you and the woman next door?"

Tag shook his head. "Ow. I mean, no."

"A dead man in the alley?" Belle asked, horrified. "Detective Wilson, I think I need that weapon for protection."

"Sorry, ma'am. It was found at the scene of a crime. Until this is resolved, everything could be important."

She responded with a wave that encompassed the roomful of debris. "You have to go through everything in this room?"

Ledbetter sighed. "Yes, ma'am."

"You're a slob." She nudged Tag. "This place is a mess."

"I didn't expect a police investigation."

"The sun will soon be up. It's almost Christmas morning! Nobody wants to spend Christmas Day picking up trash!"

"All right—I'm sorry! When this is over, I promise to change my ways."

"I should hope so!"

"We'll need to seal this apartment. Do you have someplace to stay?"

"Of course. He'll stay at my place," Belle answered.

Ledbetter's heart sank. "An officer will see you home."

She laughed. "I live across the hall, in 807. We can find the way."

"Nah—I'll go stay with my uncle. He puts out quite a Christmas spread."

"Would that be Chinese food, by any chance?" Ledbetter wondered.

"How did you guess? Oh, yeah—my shirt."

Wilson watched as Tag selected clothes to take with him. Then they all left the apartment and Ledbetter locked the door.

After Tag had walked away, Belle put a hand on Ledbetter's arm. "Detective."

His heart seemed to expand and fill his chest. "Yes."

"I don't know what your plans are for Christmas, but when you finish here, would you like to come to my place?"

Keyboard

Mark Crimmins

Straddling the Trackpad, your wrists rest on the wide flat spaces below the keyboard. Your thumbs take up their posts at the right and left ends of the Button. Both sets of fingers from little to middle position themselves on the A-S-D and K-L-; Keys. Reaching for the F and J Keys, the delicate prehensile instruments of your index fingers orient themselves to their anticipated tasks, hypersensitive tips hovering millimeters above their respective Home Keys and feeling—with the light brush of a fingerprint—for the two little upraised bars at the bottom of the keys. Drawing your right hand back you position your right index finger over the Trackpad. Next, your left thumb slides over the Trackpad and pauses, ready to strike downwards onto the Button and indeed actually slowly lowering onto the Button and resting on it but not heavily enough to depress it. Marking four points on an asymptotic curve, your left fingers are fanned in an arc across the keyboard. Your right index finger descends to the surface of the Trackpad and locates the touch-activated cursor on the screen. The finger drags the cursor, which morphs into the black arrow of the Mouse Pointer, placing it in the middle of the blue oceans bounded by Firefox's globe-gobbling vixen. The arrow pointing at the center of the Firefox icon, your thumb springs into action, clicking the left side of the Trackpad Button, the four fingers of your left hand leaping flamboyantly into the air in compensatory motion as the screen changes to the Firefox Homepage. Now your right finger darts down to the Trackpad and drags across the Trackpad to scroll the Mouse Pointer up to the top of the screen, carefully placing its tip in the middle of a blue star on the right end of the Address Bar. You move the Mouse Pointer to the left of the blue star and align it with a string of symbols you need to delete before you can type in an Internet Address. When the Mouse Pointer is aligned with the last datum, it changes back into the vertical cursor and your left thumb moves back to the Trackpad Button, presses it, and holds it down. The Trackpad Button depressed, your right index finger (its tip anyway) gently pushes the Mouse Pointer leftwards along the Address Bar, highlighting the string of symbols, the blue Highlight Bar smoothly flowing from right to left as it Hoovers up the symbols in the line. You lift your right index finger from the Trackpad and your left thumb from the Trackpad Button, stabilizing the blue bar of highlighted data. Now you describe a tiny St. Louis Arch parabola through the air with that oh so authoritative right index finger and bring it down with a satisfying tap onto the Delete Key, instantly disappearing the highlighted string of symbols and the highlight bar itself and leaving the Address Bar a beautiful empty white box ready to receive your data input. Hands moving quickly back to Home Position on the keyboard, your left second finger shoots out to the W key and taps it thrice in quick succession as your right second finger drops diagonally southeast from its home space above the L key to hit the Period Key. Now your left index finger leaps from the F Key over the G to the B Key and hits it twice, moving back immediately to its position above the F Key as your left middle finger descends from its D to the C diagonally below it. Your right index finger drops from the J to the N while your left index and second fingers move up a row to type, middle finger first, the E and the W Keys, before moving back down to home position, where your second finger taps its home key, the S. Now your right second finger drops to the period again, and your left middle finger descends to the C, moving back to Home Position as your right second finger ascends to the O. Finally, your right index finger drops down to the M while your right pinkie swoops onto the Return Key from ten inches above the board. Your preferred newspaper's Home Page flashes onto your screen. You read the large font banner headline, smile faintly, and click on the bold beautiful words.

The Best Possible Answer

Michael Webb

"I love you so much, Stephen," she says, "but right now, I want to smack that stupid look off your face."

Her eyes are brimming with tears. I try to speak. I make no sound. I feel weighted, tied to the chair, without energy or will. The dress she is wearing, a dark blue color, shows part of her shoulders, the tan skin of her neck, the shadowy dip above her collarbone that my lips know the contours of, the white innocence of a single undergarment strap. She is speaking quietly, precisely, making every word clear and sharp in the suddenly poisoned air between us.

I am thinking of a time I got high and watched 'The Godfather' movies in college with my friend Tom. Tom told me to watch Pacino very carefully, and notice how calm he always was, so that during the few times when he did lose his temper, it was doubly terrifying. Emine was like that. She cried and got angry, but she almost always did so quietly, and on the occasions when she raised her voice, it was frightening. She hadn't yet, but I was preparing for it, like a beach homeowner buttoning up before a storm.

"I mean, I told you an hour ago, and I don't think you've said five words. What the hell are you feeling? Terror? Joy? Anxiety? Fear? Anticipation? What? Whatever you're feeling, I accept it. But I insist you share with me. And don't give me that crap about theorems and results and conjectures. I don't give a shit about that stuff. I told you the first time we met that I didn't mind that I couldn't have all of you, that all I wanted was a piece. But you're not even giving me that."

I am thinking about a documentary I saw about Andrew Wiles and the solution to Fermat's Last Theorem. The filmmaker asked an American mathematician to explain why all of the filmmaker's interview subjects took an incredibly long time to answer questions. The filmmaker said he would start to worry that the question had been poorly understood, or the respondent's English perhaps was not good enough. "Mathematicians hate imprecision," the mathematician said. "They were thinking of the best possible answer to your questions."

"Jesus Christ," Emine says. She pushes her chair back and stands up. I can see her waist, where the dress narrows and then flares out again. I want to tell her stop, wait, something that will stem the tide of anger, that will make her sit down and eat her cooling ravioli, but I can't find any words that matter.

"When you're ready to talk," she says, "you know where I am." She turns and walks out of the restaurant, the dress swishing in her wake. I watch her go, unable to react, waiting for the energy, for the desire to stand, to act, wondering what the distance is between laziness and fear.

Also from Pure Slush Books

https://pureslush.com/store/

- Greed 7 Deadly Sins Vol. 3
ISBN: 978-1-925536-64-5 (paperback) / 978-1-925536-65-2 (eBook)
- Gluttony 7 Deadly Sins Vol. 2
ISBN: 978-1-925536-54-6 (paperback) / 978-1-925536-55-3 (eBook)
- Lust 7 Deadly Sins Vol. 1
ISBN: 978-1-925536-47-8 (paperback) / 978-1-925536-48-5 (eBook)
- Happy² Pure Slush Vol. 15
ISBN: 978-1-925536-39-3 (paperback) / 978-1-925536-40-9 (eBook)
- Inane Pure Slush Vol. 14
ISBN: 978-1-925536-17-1 (paperback) / 978-1-925536-18-8 (eBook)
- Freak Pure Slush Vol. 13
ISBN: 978-1-925536-15-7 (paperback) / 978-1-925536-16-4 (eBook)